GONE

Kathleen Long

Second edition 2018
SteeleHouse Press

Visit the author at kathleenlong.com

For Ellie Grogan.
A light so bright shall never be forgotten.

PLEASE NOTE

There is a temptation, when rereleasing stories written twelve years earlier, to rewrite phrasing and language to fit today's style. In reissuing my original Body Hunter trilogy, I've chosen not to update for changes in either my writing or technology. My hope is that you'll enjoy these stories—written before there was a video camera on every corner and a smart pone in every pocket—just as they are.

Happy reading.

CAST OF CHARACTERS

Will Connor—Codirector of the Body Hunters, he faked his death seventeen years ago to save the lives of those he loved. Now, when his daughter goes missing, he must take on the biggest challenge of his life—risking his heart.

Maggie Connor—She's devoted the years since her husband's sudden death to keeping her daughter sheltered and protected. When Jordan goes missing, Maggie will do whatever it takes to save her daughter's life, even if that means working alongside the man she buried seventeen years earlier.

Jordan Connor—Tired of living in a bubble, Jordan finds that her dreams of adventure come to an abrupt end when the object of her island romance turns out to be a coldhearted kidnapper.

Commissioner Dunkley—The head of the Royal Police, he's already classified Jordan Connor as a runaway, but was his decision based on fact? Or is the commissioner acting as a puppet for a far larger foe?

Diego Montoya—An international heroin smuggler, he vanished following the death of his nemesis, Will Connor. Has he come back now to finish what he started—to destroy those Will loves most?

Ferdinand King—A wealthy businessman and philanthropist, he deals in a most precious commodity—human lives.

The Body Hunters—Rick Matthews, Kyle Landenburg, Lily Christides, Julian Harris and Silvia Hellman. Dedicated to finding victims and villains society has abandoned, they'll use every means necessary to bring Jordan Connor home alive. The body clock is ticking.

PROLOGUE

Jordan Connor tossed a change of clothes into the cheap knapsack she'd bought from the street vendor in Newmarket. She glanced at the soft leather bag her mother had given her as a graduation present, regret sliding through her at the thought of leaving the prized possession behind.

She had no choice.

The less obvious she was in leaving, the more likely she was to get away with her plan.

Taylor was still sleeping, snoring softly from the four glasses of rum punch she'd downed at the bar last night. With any luck, she wouldn't notice Jordan gone for hours. That ought to be plenty of time to meet Jaime and be well out to sea. Far away from the life she'd known—and hated.

So long curfews and rules and safety tips and self-defense classes.

Her heart gave a sharp twist at the thought of her mother's reaction when she got the news Jordan had vanished, but she'd brought it on herself.

Really.

How far down could you shove a kid's spirit before she felt ready to explode?

Jordan had passed the point of combustion years ago. Senior week on Isle de Cielo had finally given her the match for her fuse. Thank God.

She checked her hair in the mirror, giving the long blond curls a quick fluff.

Jaime said she was the most beautiful woman he'd ever seen, and he should know. After all, he was thirty. He'd been around, and he'd had a lot of women. She was sure of it. How lucky was she that he'd picked her to take on his latest adventure?

Traveling the Caribbean. Different ports. Different islands. Different identities.

A thrill rippled through her and she shivered with excitement.

Her mother's plans for pharmacy school could wait.

Jordan was about to see the world—with Jaime as her guide.

She scribbled a note to Taylor. After all, they'd been best friends since first grade. Jordan had to tell her the truth.

She hesitated.

Jaime had told her not to breathe a word to anyone. Surely, he hadn't meant Taylor, had he?

She eyed the note in her hand, then the pillow beneath her friend's head. If she tucked it there, how long would it be before Taylor found it? And would Taylor keep her mouth shut, or would she tell Jordan's mother?

Maggie Connor would call out the Coast Guard—or whatever it was they had down here—to drag Jordan back.

No. Jordan gave her head a quick shake.

She crumpled the note in her hand and tossed it in the bathroom trash can.

Taylor would have to understand. That's what friends were for.

Jordan checked her knapsack one more time, pulled open the door to the hotel room her mother had paid for, and stepped out into the dark hall. Dawn had just begun to break and she had to get moving. Jaime had said launching the boat before sunrise was a vital part of their plan.

Their *plan.*

She sighed.

This was better than any book she'd ever read, and books had been the closest thing to excitement she'd gotten in a long, long time. Like forever.

Jordan pulled the door shut and made her way quickly to the staircase, then out around the pool and toward the beach.

Jaime had given her strict instructions on how to get to the boat. The fewer people she ran into the better.

All part of the plan.

When he stepped out from behind a stand of palm trees, her heart skipped.

"I thought you were going to meet me at the boat?"

She launched herself into his arms, savoring the

feel of his strong hands around her waist, thrilling to the sensation of his touch as he slid one palm up over her breast.

They hadn't yet made love, but she knew he was the one.

"There's been a change in plans, little one." He looked down into her eyes, an unfamiliar emotion swirling in the dark depths of his gaze.

He turned her, pressing her back against his stomach as she faced the shimmering Caribbean waters.

"Like what?" she asked.

"A very special side trip." He anchored his arm around her waist, pinning her arm to her side. He trailed his other hand down the side of her face, tracing the curve of her shoulder, the skin of her upper arm.

Heat ignited inside her and she leaned into him, wanting so badly for him to teach her everything. *Everything.*

When he wrapped his fingers around her elbow and squeezed so hard it hurt, a flicker of fear mixed with her excitement.

"Jaime? You're hurting me."

"You made this so easy." His warm breath brushed against her ear. "So easy."

His hand left her side long enough to shove a rag into her mouth.

Terror overtook her and she writhed against him, fighting against whatever it was he was doing.

He hoisted her into the air, and as her feet left the soft sand of the beach, confusion and panic whirled through her.

If this was his idea of a joke, it wasn't funny.

She struggled to free herself, but couldn't. What about her self-defense training? And all those years of karate?

Jordan kicked, connecting solidly with Jaime's kneecap.

"*Madre de Dios*," he swore in her ear.

He jerked her body violently, bending her like a rag doll. Pain exploded through her arm as he carried her into the nearby palms, and she wondered if he'd broken one of her bones.

Jordan bit at the gag he'd shoved in her mouth, bile rising in her throat.

Was he going to rape her? Kill her?

When he tossed her to the ground at the feet of a second man, her insides turned liquid and she clenched her muscles to keep from soiling herself.

The second man used the toe of his boot to turn her onto her back.

Tears streamed down her face, mixing with the sand and dirt that now coated her skin. She stared up into the man's scarred face and dead eyes, and she whimpered.

He knelt next to her, holding a syringe up to the dawning light, giving it a flick with one fingernail.

"There, there." He smiled, a flash of gold teeth in sharp contrast to his dark skin. "I'm going to give you something to make you go to sleep. You won't feel a thing."

She tried to roll away, but Jaime's foot came down

on her chest, pinning her to the ground. Jaime.

She'd thought he loved her. *Loved* her.

She looked up at him, meeting his dark gaze. Why? she asked with her eyes. Why?

His only response was a grin so evil and cold her heart hurt.

All these years her mother had been right. Jordan never should have left Seattle. Never should have taken this trip.

The second man pressed a hand to her upper arm, his touch hot and scratchy as the needle pricked Jordan's skin.

"With any luck at all, *querita*, your daddy will save you while you're still in one piece."

The sound of the two men's laughter echoed through her brain as she slid toward unconsciousness.

She focused on a single thought—a single, terrifying thought. Her daddy wouldn't save her. He couldn't save her.

He'd been dead for seventeen years.

CHAPTER ONE

Body Clock: 13:00

Will Connor resented Rick Matthews's interruption before the other man so much as opened his mouth.

He'd worked all day preparing the briefing session for the Body Hunters' latest case, and the key players were scheduled to arrive later that night. He needed a few more hours without interruption.

That wasn't too much to ask for, was it?

Rick nodded in Will's direction. "Need to talk."

Will leveled his gaze at his partner, frustration edging through him. "Let me get this squared away first."

The agency codirector shook his head. "Now, Will."

"Rick—"

But the other man had already walked away.

Will covered the distance between the war-room wall and the door in a few angry strides. When he found Rick waiting in the office they shared, he planned to launch into a few choice descriptions of what Rick could do with his interruptions, but the look on his friend's face stopped him cold.

"What's happened?"

He'd never seen Rick fazed by any of the cases they'd handled over the past twenty years. Not one. He and Rick had been the driving force behind the development of the Body Hunters—a group of private individuals determined to tidy up the messes law enforcement chose to leave behind.

Over those years, they'd seen it all and solved it all. Kidnappings. Serial killings. Domestic violence. Cold cases.

But this time, Rick's expression reflected an emotion Will hadn't seen there for a very long time.

Fear.

Genuine, raw fear.

"What?" Will's voice went tight.

"Coed. Vanished on Isle de Cielo early this morning."

"Runaway?" Will's investigative brain automatically clicked into gear, working the possibilities.

Rick nodded. "So the locals would like everyone to think."

"But you disagree?"

Another nod. "Too tidy. No loose ends."

"I'd call a missing girl a loose end."

"I'll give you that."

A shadow passed across Rick's face, kicking Will's curiosity into high gear.

"What do they have so far?" he asked.

"Left her possessions and passport behind. Ran away with some thirty-year-old she met on the island. Apparently she'd changed her mind about entrusting her best friend with her plans. Locals found a crumpled note in the trash when they swept the room."

"Anything else? Clues as to who this guy is?"

"Nothing. Roommate said she'd never met him, but that our victim called him Jaime."

Will released a sarcastic laugh. "That narrows it down. Nothing else?"

Rick shook his head.

"So who's to say she's not a runaway?"

Rick's expression darkened. "The note faxed to our private line not five minutes ago."

"Note?" Will's pulse quickened.

Rick handed him the single sheet of paper. "Apparently from the kidnappers."

"How—"

Will dropped his focus to the words on the page, not believing his eyes.

We meet again, Mr. Connor. The girl or you.

We meet again.

A madman's favorite greeting.

Diego Montoya.

Will's heart ground to a stop.

A name from his past—a past that had cost him

everything he loved. When Rick and Will had been closing in on Montoya's heroin operation, the drug lord had forced Will to take drastic actions to save his family.

Montoya had dropped off the radar screen not long after.

"But he's been underground as long as I have." Anger pulsed through Will.

"If this is his work, he's decided to make a comeback," Rick answered.

Will scrubbed a hand over his face, not wanting to believe what he was hearing. "No identifying characteristics on the note? Nothing we can trace as to where the fax originated?"

"Blocked."

Will reread the note. "It's obvious what he wants."

One of Rick's dark brows lifted. "You."

Will narrowed his eyes. "How does he know I'm alive?"

Rick shrugged and shook his head.

"Who's the girl?" Will asked the question, but he knew the answer.

If Montoya had resurfaced, the victim could only be one of two people. The two people in the world for whom Will would do anything, including faking his own death in order to save their lives.

A fist of dread tightened deep inside Will's gut.

Rick's gaze never left his face, never wavered.

"Recent Seattle high-school graduate. On Isle de Cielo for senior week. I confirmed her identity with the Royal Cielo Police."

The scenario played out in Will's head as if someone had flipped the switch to an old-time movie projector, sending the frames flashing through his mind's eye.

A swaddled newborn. An infant's cry. A toddler's giggle.

"It's Jordan."

Jordan.

Even though Will had known in his heart, hearing Rick speak his daughter's name sent an ice-cold dagger through his soul.

The blond-haired, blue-eyed infant he'd last seen hours before he'd "died" in a tragic explosion. He'd made no further contact with his family, never risking so much as a drive past their house or a late-night phone call just to hear one of their voices.

Will had been gone for seventeen years and he had no doubt his family had moved on with their lives.

His chest hurt, as it did whenever he thought about the possibility of his wife, Maggie, in another man's arms. Another man's bed.

Will shook his head, not willing to believe Montoya had found out he was alive.

Will had stayed where dead men stayed.

Buried.

He'd run every Body Hunters' operation from the inside, never so much as making an appearance in the field. He'd changed his name from Mack to Will, using a favorite nickname his wife had given him. As far as anyone on the team knew, he didn't have a last name.

He had no use for one.

So how had the information leaked? Had someone on the team found out about his past? Had someone they'd busted put the puzzle pieces of his life together? Had a previous client sold him out?

Will turned and slammed his fist into the wall, then spun to face Rick, who was now on his feet.

He'd given up everything to protect his wife and daughter. Everything.

"They were supposed to be safe."

Anger exploded inside him, hot fury spreading through his every muscle.

The bastard had Jordan.

He had to be stopped.

"They were. As long as Montoya thought you dead." Rick rounded his desk, stopping a few feet from where Will stood.

"We need to know who leaked this."

Rick closed his eyes as if the question caused him pain. "Maybe he tracked you all on his own." He shrugged. "Maybe he never believed you were dead. I don't know. But right now we have to find Jordan before Montoya—or whoever is behind this—finds you." He turned back to his desk. "I'm pulling our best operatives. Sending them straight to Cielo."

"No."

Rick froze, his expression puzzled.

Will patted his chest. "This one's mine. All mine. I pick the team."

"You can't go back out there. You'll be dead in less than twenty-four hours."

"Thanks for the vote of confidence, buddy, but she's

my daughter. My team."

"Then you'll want to see this." Rick slid a photograph from an envelope on his desk, extending the glossy print toward Will.

Will shook his head. "Not now."

Rick's chiseled features tightened, his dark eyes becoming determined. "Don't you think you should know what your own daughter looks like?"

Will took the photograph, steadying himself before he studied the captured image.

He stared down into a face as beautiful as her mother's. Same jawline. Same mouth. Same shimmering blond hair. Her blue eyes, however, had gone brown and were now identical to Will's. There was no mistaking the girl's parentage.

Will's throat tightened, and he shoved the photo back at Rick. "Save it for the meeting."

Rick returned the snapshot to the envelope. "I thought it best your initial reaction happen in private and not in front of the team." He rounded his desk, heading for the door. "After all, you did train every one of them." He pointed to Will's face. "And they'll read you like a book."

Waves of emotion crashed through Will's system.

Disbelief. Anger. Fear. Love.

Rick was right. He hadn't been prepared for the full impact of seeing Jordan as a young woman, but he had to keep up a calm, controlled image for the team.

He'd invested so much time—hours, days, years—convincing himself that walking out of his family's lives had been the right thing to do. Still, he'd thought about them, wondered about them, every day.

Jordan was more than the pretty baby she'd been when he vanished.

She was now a beautiful young woman. *His daughter*.

In whose hands? Montoya's?

A shudder slid down his spine as he worked to shove away the mental images of the horrors Jordan might have already endured.

He'd seen Montoya's handiwork firsthand.

Will squeezed his eyes shut, but Jordan's image remained burned into his memory.

He'd find her. Save her. Return her to Maggie.

Then he'd walk away.

Too many years had passed to do anything else.

"No one will think any less of you if you run the show from right here," Rick said. "If Montoya wants you dead, we may not be able to stop him this time."

Will shook his head. "I died once to keep my daughter safe." He turned and headed back toward the war room, mentally preparing himself to put together the most important briefing of his life.

He paused at the door, looked back over his shoulder and forced a grim smile. "I'm not afraid to die again."

"What if she's already dead?" Rick asked, verbalizing the question Will would have asked first had this been any other kidnapping. But it wasn't. This was his daughter.

"Not a possibility."

"You have to look at this thing from all sides. What

if he never meant to let her live?" Rick asked. "Never meant to hand her over?"

"Then he's more ruthless now than he ever was, but he's forgotten something."

"What?"

"I'm more ruthless than he'll ever be."

Body Clock: 30:45

MAGGIE CONNOR white-knuckled the armrest as she stared out the jetliner window.

Water spanned below her as far as the eye could see, but her mind was focused elsewhere.

Isle de Cielo.

Her insides pitched sideways and she reached for the airsickness bag, eliciting a worried glance from the man one seat over. She left the bag tucked into the pocket in front of her, willing herself to keep down the ginger ale she'd sipped during the first leg of her flight.

The pilot announced the plane's descent toward the island. A vacation paradise, her daughter had told her. Safe, she'd promised.

Maggie mentally berated herself for the millionth time since she'd received Taylor's panicked phone call.

Jordan was gone.

She'd vanished, supposedly running away with a man she'd met during her vacation.

Maggie had flown all night to make it to the island from Seattle.

She pressed her fingertips to her pounding temples.

What had she been thinking, letting Jordan go alone? Well, not entirely alone, but going with Taylor didn't count for much more. The two had been as one since first grade.

If Maggie had been smart, she'd have insisted on going herself, but she'd barely left the house since Will's death. Going to Cielo would have been a huge leap out of her comfort zone.

She laughed.

Going to Cielo *was* a huge leap out of her comfort zone.

She traced a finger over the scrap of paper onto which she'd written the contact information for the Royal Cielo Police. She'd done so too many times to count over the past twenty-four hours.

Commissioner Dunkley had tried to calm her fears over the phone, assuring her Jordan would return home safe and sound after the bloom of her newly found romance faded.

A runaway.

Never, Maggie screamed silently. Jordan would never run away. Would she?

Maggie replayed the last seventeen years in her mind, starting with Will's funeral—a funeral which had been delayed for two weeks due to her own accident.

She absentmindedly traced the scar that rimmed her eye and cut into the line of her cheekbone. A few more inches and Jordan would have been an orphan before her first birthday.

Maggie had been so intent on reaching the scene of

the explosion that had claimed Will's life, she'd never seen the stop sign.

Will's best friend and partner, Rick Matthews, had stayed by her side, had filled in the blanks, had tried to coax her out of the shell into which she'd retreated on that fateful day, but she'd wanted no part of the outside world. Wanted no part of life or love or friendship.

She and Rick had lost touch over the years. Last Maggie had heard, he'd sold the trade-show business he and Will had built from the ground up. She'd received a check for her share of the profits. There'd been nothing more in the envelope.

No note.

No correspondence.

It was better that way.

She blew out a sigh and fought the fear clawing at her throat, her fingertips itching to hold the airsickness bag just in case.

What if Jordan had been kidnapped? Or worse?

What if Maggie was already too late?

There were countless places in the Caribbean for Jordan to hide, or for someone to hide her.

Maggie hadn't the slightest idea of where to start looking. She wasn't a detective. She hadn't been much of anything the past seventeen years except an overprotective mother.

An overprotective mother who had failed her daughter when push came to shove.

The plane's landing gear sent an unforgiving jolt through the cabin, shaking Maggie's thoughts back into focus.

Jordan had taken this same flight.

Perhaps the place to start was with retracing every step her daughter had taken. She was counting on Taylor—waiting at the hotel for her arrival—to help her do just that.

But first, Maggie needed to pay a visit to Commissioner Dunkley. She fingered the slip of paper once more.

The man might not share her conviction that Jordan wasn't a runaway, but she'd make damned sure he shared every piece of information he'd gathered.

A good half hour later, she sat in his office, amazed at how little information there was to share.

The police had been so dead set on Jordan being a runaway they'd pursued the case no further than the hotel room and the surrounding area.

"The hotel manager saw your daughter leave, Mrs. Connor."

Maggie snapped her attention from where she'd been staring at a worn spot on the carpet to the commissioner's face, her heart beating a bit quicker at the man's words. "He did?"

The man nodded, his dark eyes soft with kindness. "*She* did. Your daughter left of her own free will. I'm sorry."

Her own free will.

Maggie's vision blurred and she blinked to clear away her tears, not wanting this man to see her fear, to sense her desperation. But that's exactly what she was.

Desperate.

If she'd lost Jordan, she'd lost everything. First Will. Now Jordan. Heaven knew she'd given up any attempts at a life of her own years ago. Everything she'd done, said, worked for since Will's death, she'd done only for Jordan.

She'd fought to keep her safe, keep her fed, keep her buffered behind the walls of their home.

She'd relented only once, to let Jordan take this trip. Look where that decision had gotten them.

"I'd like to see my daughter's case file, please." Maggie forced a note of calm into her voice that in no way reflected the turmoil she felt inside.

"I assure you, Mrs. Connor, your daughter will be back before you know it. I've seen this happen many, many times before." Slight wrinkles formed around the man's eyes as he offered her a superficial smile.

If he thought he could smile and put her mind at ease, he needed to think again.

She shook her head. "And I assure you, Commissioner Dunkley, my daughter did not run away. She's not capable of doing something so foolish."

His dark brows lifted toward his hairline. "We parents are often surprised by what our children are capable of. Perhaps you'll feel differently after a short rest."

Anger surged inside her now, heat spreading upward to her neck and cheeks. The commissioner took a backward step, as if he knew she was about to lose all semblance of emotional control.

Maggie jammed a finger into his chest, the move

completely uncharacteristic of the quiet, withdrawn woman she'd become.

"*You* do not know my daughter. *I* know my daughter. And I will investigate her disappearance with or without your help. Am I making myself clear?"

He nodded, his features turning grim.

"Do not think your phony pity or condescension will placate me," she continued. "It won't."

A slight smile pulled at the corners of his mouth, the resulting expression more chilly than comforting.

"And do not think your words will threaten me, Mrs. Connor. We have done our job here, and the case is closed. The file is closed."

He stepped away from her touch. "I understand you're upset, and you have my deepest sympathies. My driver will take you to your hotel. Your daughter's friend is waiting for you there."

He turned and left the small office before Maggie could utter another word, leaving her stunned by his rapid transition from caring to cold.

The case is closed.

The man's words echoed through her brain even as his driver appeared in the doorway of the small room, beckoning for her to follow him outside.

Maggie did so, putting one foot in front of the other without conscious thought or effort.

The file is closed.

Over my dead body, Maggie thought. She shook her head, determination welling inside her.

For the briefest moment she wished Will were by

her side—always calm, always logical Will with his love of mysteries. If anyone would be able to piece together what had happened here, it would be Will.

Maggie gave herself a mental shake.

Having Will by her side would never be a possibility again.

She was fully and completely alone. She should be used to the feeling.

Only now, her daughter was gone without any trace other than a handwritten note.

The hotel manager had seen her walk away.

The commissioner's words ran through her head as the driver pulled out onto the road and headed down the lushly landscaped road away from the police station toward her hotel.

The lead wasn't much, but it was all she had. She'd start her investigation there then go forward.

Maggie had no idea of what she was doing, but she couldn't afford a single mistake.

Jordan's life depended on it.

HE WATCHED as the car carrying the woman left the parking lot and disappeared out onto the road. "Do you think she'll be a problem?" He turned to measure Dunkley's expression.

"No."

He questioned the commissioner's response with a simple lift of his eyebrows.

"You have my word on it," Dunkley added. "I'll see to it that she finds nothing."

He turned toward the hall, headed toward the back

entrance. "You'll be rewarded handsomely when all is said and done."

He paused, adding one last thought before he stepped outside. "I'm sure I don't need to tell you the price you'll pay should you fail."

"I won't fail you."

"Very well."

But as he dropped into the driver's seat of his car and cranked the ignition, an unsettled feeling took root deep inside him.

He hadn't counted on the mother appearing on the island, only the father. He'd planned for the latter. The former was a complete surprise. His intelligence had told him the mother never set foot outside Seattle.

Hell, she never set foot outside her house.

If she had to be taken care of, he'd have no problem doing so. Collateral damage had never slowed him down in the past. This time would be no different.

At long last his plans were coming to fruition. He wasn't about to let some reclusive housewife from Seattle get in his way.

If she got too close to the truth, she'd vanish.

Just like her beloved daughter.

CHAPTER TWO

Body Clock: 31:50

Will stood at the whiteboard, taking a moment to study the faces seated in the small jet as they winged their way toward Isle de Cielo.

The Body Hunters' willingness to drop their public lives for their very private missions never ceased to amaze him. And, more than likely, he hadn't appreciated the full magnitude of their work until this moment.

Until the missing *body* was none other than his daughter.

He'd handpicked the team, and not one balked at the idea of grabbing a change of clothes, a passport and heading out of Seattle, leaving their families, their jobs, their lives behind.

They'd boarded the Body Hunters' jet in the middle of the night and had each grabbed what sleep they could, knowing sleep would be a rare commodity in the days to come.

Now that they were within two hours of their arrival, Will was ready to begin the briefing—the Body Case, as they called it.

The Body Hunters operated with one mission: to bring home the body. Alive.

He watched the team now as they settled into their seats, moving amongst each other with an ease and familiarity brought on by years of working together.

Lily Christides, one of the younger members of the team, had proven to be a natural at tracking funds and key players in the international market. She also had a keen ability to cut right to the meat of any discussion or interview. Her honesty more than made up for what she lacked in tact.

Lily pulled her long brown hair back into a ponytail as she dropped into the empty seat next to Kyle Landenburg. She spoke softly to Kyle even as she reached down for the cup of coffee he'd left waiting for her in the seat's drink holder.

Kyle sipped on his own steaming cup, listening to Lily, but never taking his eyes from Will, no doubt wondering just what Will was doing on the outside.

Kyle boasted a tough-as-nails exterior. Military training. Peak physical conditioning. Six-foot- five and nothing but muscle. Piercing blue eyes and hair cropped so close to his skull Will often wondered why Kyle didn't just shave his head.

He was twice the size of Lily. The brawn to her beauty. Yet, the two of them had forged a friendship that had proven invaluable in the field. They regularly anticipated each other's moves, understood each other's thoughts and shortcomings.

Will had once wondered whether or not there might be romantic interest between the two, but he'd quickly realized his mistake. Kyle looked at Lily with nothing but protectiveness in his gaze. Theirs was a friendship built on trust and respect, nothing more.

Kyle frowned and Will wondered if he already had a hint about what had happened.

Rick and Will were the only members of the team to know Kyle was intuitive, something the burly man chose not to make public, and a skill that had brought Kyle much heartache.

He'd ignored the ability at first, including the intuition that his wife was about to walk into an armed bank robbery. Without warning, Sally Landenburg had left home to make a savings account deposit and she'd never come back.

Kyle had dedicated himself to helping save others from heartache ever since. He freelanced in security and self-defense training, but the majority of his waking hours were spent at the base, poring over files of missing and wanted individuals.

Silvia Hellman sat in the front row of chairs, stitching on a small square. Will knew exactly what she was doing without looking closer. The tiny senior might be a whiz when it came to research, and was an invaluable resource for the team during active cases, but she occupied herself with a far gentler pursuit in her downtime.

She quilted.

Will couldn't think of a single missing persons case for which Silvia hadn't made a quilt, always believing they'd find the body alive. On the rare occasion they didn't, she presented the quilt to the family, a loving gesture of kindness.

The only people missing from the briefing were Rick, who'd run to his private quarters to grab something, and Julian Harris, the newest member of their team.

To the outside world, Julian was an outgoing pharmaceutical company executive. To the members of the team, he was a driven truth seeker, deeply affected by the death of a cousin who'd gotten hold of tainted heroin.

Julian had been out of the country negotiating for the purchase of raw materials for his company when word of Jordan's disappearance reached Rick and Will.

They'd sent him ahead to Isle de Cielo with explicit instructions on getting the safe house ready for the team's arrival.

"We have a situation on Isle de Cielo," Rick said as he rounded the doorway. "If you're all settled, Will's prepared to brief you. Will?"

Will took a moment to let everyone focus, then he began.

"As you may or may not have figured out, I'm taking the lead on this body."

Kyle's forehead wrinkled. "No offense, Will, but you haven't been in the field in years."

"No." Will thinned his lips as he pressed Jordan's

photo up to the board along with a map of Isle de Cielo. "But back in the day, Rick and I ran every mission. Just the two of us. I know what I'm doing."

He pointed toward the map of the island, tapping a finger against the west coast.

"We have a seventeen-year-old female missing from a medium-budget resort hotel. Roommate states the girl had taken up with a thirty-year-old male during the week prior to her disappearance. Royal Cielo Police found a crumpled note stating the girl's departure was voluntary."

"Runaway?" Kyle asked, his mind obviously sorting through the facts as Will detailed them.

Will shook his head. "It would appear so on the surface, but contact has been made by someone claiming to be the kidnapper."

Lily blew out a soft sigh and Kyle's expression shifted, his features going flat. He knew there was more here than an anonymous missing coed.

"Who's the body?" he asked.

Leave it to Kyle to skip the pleasantries.

Will had always assumed the group's use of the word *body* to refer to their current case might offend outsiders. Yet, until today, he hadn't thought twice about using the term. Today, however, the word sounded cold and unfeeling when he felt anything but.

He hesitated, taking a step away from the board. "My daughter."

Shocked silence grew thick inside the small cabin. A chorus of mumbled condolences filled the void then faded just as quickly as they'd sounded.

The fact no one asked why they'd never heard about Will's daughter before today spoke volumes about the group's trust level.

They operated on a need-to-know basis. If neither Will nor Rick offered anything additional, the information wasn't needed. Not yet.

"How many hours?" Kyle asked.

Smart, Will thought. The man never stopped running the facts and possible outcomes. "Closing in on thirty-two," he answered.

If possible, the resulting silence was even more profound than it had been following Will's last revelation.

Each team member knew the implication of the time frame, yet not one uttered their worst fear out loud.

For that, Will was grateful.

"All right," Lily broke the awkward quiet. "Where do we start, Will? Let's get this show on the road and let's get your daughter home. Safe and sound."

Will's mouth curved into a tight but grateful smile. She might often ask too many questions, but the woman had a knack for smoothing over rough moments.

Yet, she knew as well as Will did that everyone in the room was thinking the same thing.

At almost thirty-two hours since Jordan Connor's disappearance, the harsh reality of the situation stared them all in the face.

Chances were Jordan Connor might already be

dead.

The Body Hunters would bring her home nonetheless.

After all, it's what they did.

"What do the kidnappers want?" Lily asked.

Silence beat again through the small space before Will answered.

"They want me."

MAGGIE SAT on the bed her daughter had slept in just two nights earlier and stared slack-jawed at Taylor. Her daughter's best friend had just described Jordan's whirlwind love affair with a man more than ten years her senior, and Maggie was finding it all a bit surreal.

How could the daughter she'd raised in a protective bubble have gotten herself involved with a thirty-year-old man?

Anger and fear tangled inside her.

Maybe it was the protective bubble that had caused Jordan to act out—to seek adventure. Maggie hadn't delivered any stay-away-from-stranger speeches before Jordan and Taylor set out for their graduation trip. She hadn't thought it necessary.

How wrong she'd been.

"I'm sure she'll be fine, Mrs. Connor. She'll come home soon, you'll see."

Taylor twirled a piece of long auburn hair and visibly worked to force calm into her voice, for Maggie's benefit, no doubt. Yet the stark fear plastered across her features was undeniable.

She believed her words about as much as Maggie

did.

If Jordan were fine, they'd have heard something from her by now. Her guilty conscience would have overpowered the victorious feeling of being free and independent.

Jordan would never leave Maggie hanging high and dry. Never. She'd watched the toll Will's death had taken on Maggie. His loss had been an ever-present specter in their lives.

Jordan would never go missing without an explanation.

She wasn't wired that way.

One half hour later, Maggie ran a brush through her hair and smoothed the front of her shirt. She'd put Taylor in a cab headed for the airport with explicit instructions to focus on nothing but getting home safely. Her parents would be meeting her in Seattle.

Talking to Taylor had proven to be useless, except for one thing. Maggie realized just how naive her daughter truly was. If she'd taken up with the mystery thirty-year-old without so much as a second thought, heaven only knew what else might happen to her.

Maggie headed for the resort's lobby, determined to find the hotel manager. If she'd seen Jordan walk away, perhaps she'd be able to offer additional information.

How had she looked? How had she been dressed? Had she been carrying a bag? After all, the leather weekender Maggie had given Jordan as a graduation present had been left in her room.

A frisson of unease shifted through Maggie as she headed for the office door. Once upon a time, she'd been a confident, professional woman, but over the past seventeen years she'd withdrawn. She could admit it. It didn't take a psychiatrist to tell her she'd shut down and shut out the rest of the world.

She steeled herself as she stood in front of the door, fist poised to knock.

The time had come to let the rest of the world back in.

"Mrs. Connor?"

Maggie spun on one heel, searching for the face that went with the voice. She locked eyes with a young man who approached her, hand outstretched.

"I'm Eileen's assistant, Fran. Eileen sends her apologies. She's tied up in meetings with the parent company until late afternoon. She'll find you then. In the meantime, I've been instructed to get you anything you need."

Maggie thanked Fran, but headed outside, not in the mood for food or drink or anything else at that moment. She wanted one thing and one thing only.

Information.

As she walked along the deserted stretch of beach, the sound of happy laughter and chatter rang out from the seating area for the resort's restaurant.

How could anyone eat at a time like this?

Jordan had vanished without a trace and the local police seemed unwilling to concern themselves with her disappearance.

She longed to throw her arms to the sky and scream

at them all. Couldn't they see her world had shifted on its axis? Couldn't they see that life should not be going on as if nothing had happened?

Was Maggie blowing the entire thing out of proportion? No one else seemed to share her sense of urgency or dread. What if she was wrong and the police were right?

What if Jordan had run away of her own free will?

Maggie could still feel the smooth leather of Jordan's expensive bag beneath her fingertips.

Discarded. Just like her passport and most of her clothing.

Had she simply left the bag and her belongings behind and walked away from the resort? Walked away from her life?

Maggie squeezed her eyes shut, willing herself to remain rational.

Jordan would not run away. Someone had taken her, or something had gone wrong. Horribly, horribly wrong.

Maggie's steps faltered in the soft sand.

There was nothing innocent about what had happened to Jordan. Even if she'd left Isle de Cielo of her own volition, she'd done so in the company of a thirty-year-old man.

The girl was a minor, no matter how mature she claimed to be, no matter how ready to take on life she'd become during the past year.

If Maggie had to press charges based on Jordan's age, she would. Surely that would make the police stand up and take notice.

Yet no one had seen the man. No one had a description or a name. Not even Taylor.

For all intents and purposes, Jordan had vanished into thin air.

The sun had begun to slip lower in the crystal-clear Caribbean sky. Beautiful. Peaceful. Belying everything Maggie felt as emotions tumbled wildly through her.

Jordan's disappearance had brought back the unwanted memories of the day Will had died.

The phone call. The shock. The accident. The blur of her own recovery time. The funeral. The emotional and physical scars she carried still.

Tears stung at the back of her eyelids and she blinked rapidly, sinking to her knees in the cool, sugary sand.

She hugged herself, letting her chin drop to her chest, letting the tears fall.

No one would see her.

No one would care.

No one had cared for a very long time.

"She didn't want to go, ma'am."

The raspy voice startled Maggie, jolting her to attention. She lifted her gaze to meet that of an older man, small in stature, his skin weathered by years in the sun, his eyes kind, concerned.

He wore nothing but a pair of shorts, and to any passerby he'd appear to be nothing more than a man out for a casual stroll. His words suggested he was anything but.

"What did you say?" Maggie forced the words

through a tight throat.

"The girl." He nodded, pursing his lips. "She didn't want to go."

AS THEIR JET made its way south toward the island, Will continued the team briefing.

"Our primary suspect is Diego Montoya." Will pinned an outdated head shot of Montoya on the bulletin board he'd lowered from the jet's ceiling.

"But Montoya dropped off the radar screen years ago," Silvia offered. "His entire organization fell apart after you two blew his distribution network apart." She nodded to Will and Rick.

Kyle scowled. "Why come back now?"

Will hesitated for a split second and Rick pushed out of his seat, stepping to his side.

"Revenge," he said in his typically clipped tone. "The Will you know was formerly known as Mack Connor."

No one uttered a word and Rick plunged ahead. Will let him.

"Will and I carefully staged his death in order to save the lives of his wife and child." He tapped Jordan's picture where it hung from the board. "Jordan Connor and her mother Maggie.

"Diego Montoya was our prime target in those days and we'd just shut down his largest distribution route. To say the man was livid would be the understatement of the century. He blamed his failure on Mack—or Will, as you know him. He planned to hit Will where it hurt the most."

"His family." Lily spoke the words so softly they were barely audible.

Rick nodded. "So we copycatted a serial bomber from those days and took Will out of commission. Maggie and Jordan were left alone and grieving, but they lived on. The serial bomber was so upset at our imitation of his work that he slipped up. The police had him in custody within the week."

"A win-win." Will laughed bitterly.

Rick slipped the note they'd received earlier out of the case folder, handing it to Silvia to pass to the others. "If this note is valid, Montoya is back in action. While this isn't signed, it bears all the hallmarks of Montoya's mode of operation."

"An old score to settle on a new frontier." The deep rumble of Kyle's voice filled the plane.

"Apparently so," Will answered, stepping close to where the team sat, wanting them to feel fully the sincerity of what he was about to say. "But this time, I intend to make sure the man never gets another chance to come after my family. Understood?"

"Understood." Kyle's expression turned intense. "We won't let you down, Will."

The pilot announced their imminent arrival in Isle de Cielo. Will and Rick took their seats.

Moments later, as everyone gathered their belongings and headed for the exit, Silvia reached for Will's arm.

"I'll start her quilt." She gave his elbow a sharp squeeze.

"I always tell you to wait, don't I?" Will hated himself at that moment. Hated that he went into every case with a frisson of doubt at the back of his mind.

Silvia nodded. "You do. And this time?"

Will grimaced, shaking his head. "I'm not saying anything."

Silvia headed for the door as Will packed up the case file contents. From this point forward, every action he took would impact whether or not his daughter lived to celebrate her eighteenth birthday.

If she'd lived this far.

"What's her favorite color?" Silvia hesitated momentarily, one hand on the railing to the exit staircase.

Will stopped what he was doing, dropping his chin momentarily before he lifted his gaze to meet Silvia's expectant stare.

His answer was short. Honest. And it ripped him to the core.

"I have no idea."

JORDAN STRUGGLED to open her eyes, her lids sticking together momentarily as if she'd slept for days. She battled to move her tongue, working to pry apart her parched mouth.

What had happened? Where was she?

Darkness greeted her and she blinked repeatedly to clear the fog that coated her eyes and thoughts.

A vision of Jaime flashed through her mind. Laughing. Hateful. Hurtful.

Her heart ached in her chest.

Why had he done this? If he thought her family

had money, he was wrong. She and her mother had scraped to get by for as long as Jordan could remember.

And what had the other man said about her father?

Jordan reached involuntarily for the cord around her neck, sucking in a sharp breath when her fingers met nothing but bare flesh.

The necklace. Her father's wedding band.

Gone.

Emotion squeezed at her throat.

He never wore it to his basketball games, exactly where he'd been headed the day he died.

Her father's wedding band had been her talisman ever since she'd first put it around her neck at age ten. Without it...well...without it things couldn't get much worse, or seem much bleaker.

She studied her surroundings, but there wasn't much to see.

What looked like stone walls closed in on all four sides, and other than the slab of wood on which she'd been left, the room sat empty.

Completely empty.

Jordan sat up, realizing she wasn't bound in any way, and hugged herself. The air felt mild and heavy. She listened, but heard nothing.

A shudder raced through her.

Had Jaime left her here to die?

A shimmer of light played against the dirt floor near one corner of the chamber and Jordan frowned. Light? From what?

She tipped back her chin, scrutinizing the ceiling,

then spotted the light's source. A hole, complete with a perfect view of a cloudless sky.

She stood, stretching her arms as far as she could. Even so, her reach wasn't anywhere close to the ceiling or the hole that towered above her.

An escape without access. A glimpse of the freedom she might never have again.

The freedom she'd had with her mother as much as Jordan had complained she'd had no freedom at all.

All those years her mother had spent protecting her had been for what? For this?

To die in some hole like a trapped animal just because she'd been stupid enough to think a man like Jaime had been attracted to her.

How could she have been so careless?

Instead of living up to expectations, she'd lived down to the level of her mother's worst fear.

She'd forgotten every second of self-defense training as soon as the man paid her the slightest attention.

Jordan stared again at the blue sky beyond the confines of her cell's ceiling. She traced her finger over the spot on her throat where her father's band usually lay.

The gap in the ceiling was round. Just like her father's wedding band.

In that instant, Jordan decided maybe there was hope after all. If just one person saw that hole, she'd be rescued.

One person. No more.

But if Taylor had found the crumpled-up note, no one would think Jordan was anywhere but off on some yacht with Jaime.

No matter. If no one came, she'd think of something else. She hadn't suffered through years of training to die like this, let alone at her age.

Nope. She would not give up. No matter what Jaime and the man with the needle wanted.

And then Jordan Connor did something she hadn't done since she was a little girl hoping against hope for her daddy to come back from Heaven.

She prayed.

CHAPTER THREE

Body Clock: 33:15

"**S**he didn't want to go."

The man's words sent Maggie off balance and she fell back against her heels. He reached for her, steadying her by lightly grasping her elbow.

"Who are you?" she asked.

He pressed a finger to his lips and smiled. "I live in the shadows." He waved a hand dismissively. "I learned a long time ago how to go unnoticed, but I see things."

Maggie swallowed down the lump of fear and hope in her throat. "And you saw my daughter?"

He smiled again, shaking his head as he pushed to his feet. "She fought them, ma'am." He continued to shake his head as he turned to walk away. "She fought them."

"Wait." Maggie scrambled to her feet, racing to catch up to the man. "Them? What did you see?" He hesitated without turning to face her.

"Can you describe them?" Maggie's voice rang with desperation. "Anything, anything at all. Height, weight, age. Would you recognize them?"

The man's features fell flat. "The first man held her while the second man gave her the shot. She lost her ring."

"Ring?" Jordan didn't wear a ring, unless it was new. A gift from her boyfriend perhaps?

He nodded, walking away from Maggie again, putting space between them.

"I told the police officer who asked questions. He told me to keep it."

A fresh wave of shock hit Maggie like an oncoming train. "What?"

"I left it for you in your room. You should have it."

Maggie stood dumbfounded as the man walked away, then she shook herself out of her shocked trance.

"Wait a minute," she called out. "You're telling me the police know you saw something and they didn't care?"

The man did nothing but shrug his hands up into the air.

"Where can I find you? What is your name? You have to come with me to the commissioner's office."

She was a woman beyond desperation. She was downright crazed with the determination to find her daughter, and she needed to press this man for every detail she could.

Had he truly seen Jordan?

"Are you sure it was my daughter?"

"My name's Sonny, ma'am." He turned at last, the skin crinkled around his pale eyes. "I'll be in touch."

With that, he broke into a jog and disappeared into the trees.

Maggie stood her ground for several long moments, wondering if she'd imagined the encounter. Perhaps she'd gone mad.

But then she forced herself to take action.

She turned, scrambling in the soft sand, running, sliding, moving as quickly as she could back toward her room inside the complex.

I left it for you in your room.

If Will were alive he'd think her insane to chase the words of a random stranger, but Maggie was desperate. Desperate for any scrap of information she could find about Jordan's disappearance.

Perhaps a rational person would call Commissioner Dunkley and tell him everything that had just happened, but at that moment, Maggie felt anything but rational.

If the man was telling the truth, the investigating officer already knew about Jordan's struggle on the beach...and he hadn't cared.

A well-dressed woman in her late thirties stepped to her side as Maggie dashed past the manager's office.

"Normally, I'd fuss at you to rinse your feet before you make a mess of my tile work." She extended a hand, her features breaking into a warm smile. "Eileen Caldwell. I'm sorry I wasn't available to greet you earlier. I'm so sorry about your daughter."

Maggie skidded to a stop, taking in Eileen's kind expression, her casual tousle of brown hair, her sun kissed skin. Even though she wore a navy suit with white pin-stripes, the woman's stance and expression made it obvious she was very comfortable in her role.

"Commissioner Dunkley said you saw her?" Maggie asked, skipping all pleasantries.

Eileen Caldwell winced. "I'm only sorry I didn't question where your daughter was headed that early in the morning, Mrs. Connor."

"Please—" Maggie wrapped her arms around herself and shook her head "—call me Maggie."

"Maggie." Eileen nodded, offering a tight smile.

Eileen pointed toward the edge of the sparkling turquoise water, in the direction from which Maggie had just returned. "She was headed that way. I didn't wait around to see where she went." She shook her head. "I thought she might be taking an early-morning walk, but I suppose I'd have questioned the backpack she wore if only I'd had my morning coffee."

"Backpack?" Maggie's pulse quickened. *Had* Jordan truly run away?

Eileen nodded. "Another reason the police are convinced she chose to leave. Between that and the note, you can't blame them."

Maggie nodded her agreement even as her mind swirled with countless possibilities of what had happened.

"A man approached me on the beach—"

Eileen reached forward and gripped Maggie's arm. "Are you all right?"

Maggie shook her head. "It wasn't like that. He said he saw Jordan struggle with two men. Said she didn't want to go. Said he left something of hers in my room. Something he found on the beach."

Eileen stepped between Maggie and the doorway that led to her room. "We need to call the police. What if he was involved? What if whatever he left is —"

Dread flashed across the woman's features and Maggie shook her head.

"He said it was a ring."

"Ring?"

Maggie nodded, emotion spiraling into a tight knot inside her.

"Surely the police would have found something like that if it had been anywhere on that beach." Eileen's features tensed, her lips thinned. "They did search. I'm not sure if you knew that."

Maggie arched a brow. "What if they talked to the witness but told him to keep what he found?"

She locked gazes with Eileen, trying to get a read on just whose side the woman had taken.

Eileen nodded slowly. "You're right. They no doubt decided she'd run away before they came out here to ask questions. They'd assume whatever this person found had nothing to do with your daughter's case." She stepped toward the hallway to Maggie's room. "I'll check your room with you."

"You don't need to—"

"But I want to." Eileen interrupted Maggie just as they reached her door.

Maggie slowed as she inserted her room key, suddenly afraid of what she might find. And what if she found nothing at all? What if the man on the beach had made up his entire story to raise the hopes of a frightened mother?

"Want me to do that?" Eileen asked.

"No." Maggie shook her head, steeling herself.

She waited for the light to flash green, then pushed inside, noting instantly that nothing had been touched. The soft gauze curtains at the French doors fluttered a bit in the sea breeze.

Eileen crossed to the open door, checking the lock on the screen door. "You left the door like this?"

Maggie nodded as Eileen turned to await her answer. "I figured it was safe." She stumbled on the word, realizing what she'd said. She of all people, a woman who had never trusted anyone. She chuckled under her breath, muttering. "Safe."

Eileen closed the space between them. "It is safe here. Trust me. But if your daughter left not of her own free will, you have my word I'll fight this thing beside you."

Doubt flickered to life inside Maggie. Doubt and suspicion. "Why would you do that?"

Color fired in Eileen's cheeks. "Because I love this island and I love this resort. I won't let anyone tarnish our reputation."

"Oh, so it's got nothing to do with—"

Eileen pressed her palm to Maggie's arm, cutting

off her thought. "If someone I loved vanished, I'd certainly hope someone would help me out in the same situation. Got it?"

Maggie nodded, grateful, but she couldn't tear her gaze from Eileen's. Something shimmered deep inside her kind brown eyes.

She understood Maggie's pain. If Maggie didn't know better, she'd swear Eileen had lost someone she loved at some point in her past.

"What made you take this job?" Maggie asked. "You sound as though you're from the States."

"Pittsburgh," Eileen answered with a soft laugh. "Let's just say I came here on vacation and never went home." She hoisted her chin, glancing around the bright room. "Anything out of place? Anything here that wasn't here before?"

Maggie frowned, studying every inch of the living area. The blue-and-white bedspread sat untouched. The night-stand stood just as she'd left it right down to the half-full glass of water sitting next to the phone.

The doors to the patio, the dresser, everything appeared as they had been when she left the room.

Additionally, nothing had been left for her.

Maggie crossed to the bathroom, taking stock of every item on the vanity. No ring. Not anywhere.

She made no show of hiding her disappointment.

"I'm afraid there will be people who try to take advantage of your situation." Eileen placed a palm to Maggie's shoulder. "I'm sorry."

"But why would he say he found a ring?" Maggie

mentally chided herself at the blatant note of desperation in her voice.

"Did he describe it?" Eileen's eyes widened.

Maggie shook her head.

Eileen reached for the door. "I'll leave you alone now, but I'm sending over some tea. You look as though you could use a cup."

Maggie forced a grateful smile. The moment the door clicked shut behind Eileen she closed and locked the patio doors then sank into the softness of the bed, wishing there were a way to instantaneously transport herself back to Seattle.

She didn't belong here. If the police said her daughter ran away, that's probably what had happened, much as Maggie couldn't bear the thought.

The man on the beach had been the lowest of the low, concocting the false hope that Maggie had her first lead. A witness. A struggle.

She pulled a pillow away from the headboard and wrapped her arms around the softness, squeezing it tightly to her chest.

What she wouldn't give to hold her daughter this close again.

She blew out a sigh, her emotions a tangle of loss, fear, frustration and impatience. How could she let herself believe the man? She knew better.

Lord, if she believed a stranger this quickly, no wonder Jordan had put her trust in some older man. All the years of training and caution had been for nothing.

Nothing.

Maggie tossed the pillow against the headboard, pushing away from the bed. Something small and hard hit the wooden floor, stopping her cold.

Maggie dropped to her knees and followed the sound, her breath catching at the sight of the gold band where it lay, apparently having fallen from beneath the pillow or from inside the pillowcase.

She reached for the small circle, savoring the cold weight of the ring in her hand.

Will's ring. She'd know it anywhere.

When the man had said he'd found a ring, Maggie hadn't thought of Will's ring, the ever-present reminder of what might have been.

Tears stung at her eyes.

Damn the man for dying on her. And damn him for not being here now when she needed him most.

She sank back onto her heels and cradled the gold band in her palm.

The old man, Sonny, had been telling the truth. Had someone ripped the cord from Jordan's throat? Or had she lost the ring during the struggle?

A wave of nausea rolled through Maggie as she pictured her beautiful daughter in a life-and-death struggle.

"Where are you?" she spoke out loud, staring at the gold band as if it held all the answers she sought.

But then Maggie realized the ring did hold the answer she needed most. The ring told her where to start. Maggie needed to get Sonny and his description of the struggle and the men to Commissioner Dunkley.

The investigating officer might not have had an interest in the story, but surely Dunkley would.

Maggie slid the ring into the pocket of her slacks and raced for the door, stopping short when she spotted a hastily scribbled note tucked beneath the door's edge.

By now you've found the ring. Let's meet. New-market. Cielo Café. Six o'clock.

Sonny had said he'd be in touch, and apparently he was a man of his word. Yet Maggie had no intention of going into the meeting alone.

She reached for the door and headed out the back way, not wanting Eileen to spot her on the move.

Commissioner Dunkley had been less than warm when they'd parted company earlier that afternoon, so Maggie had no doubt he'd be less than happy to see her pay a return visit.

Quite frankly, she couldn't care less about the man's moods or personal opinions.

She needed Dunkley to do one thing, and one thing only.

She needed him to listen. Whether he wanted to or not.

WILL TOSSED his duffel bag onto the bed and grimaced. Brightly colored curtains fluttered at the window, and the turquoise-blue of the Caribbean Sea sparkled just fifty yards away.

Someone had turned back the delicate white bedspread, showing off linens that matched the window treatments and contrasted sharply with the black wrought-iron headboard.

The room was a far cry from the rooms in which he and Rick had crashed during the early days of their investigating. That much was certain. During those times, more often than not, they'd have erected a lean-to for shelter on an island such as this one, wanting to stay out of sight of local authorities.

He and Rick had long since leveraged funds from the sale of their private business to allow them to run the agency in first-class style.

Will had heard stories about this particular safe house, however. Beneath the stylish beachside bungalow hid an operations center like no other.

Julian had been here on a previous mission and had assured Will and Rick they wouldn't be disappointed.

Will was sure they wouldn't be. He'd trained Julian personally, and while he might be relatively new to the Body Hunters' way of life, the young man was sharp and smart. A natural.

Will crossed toward the ornate mirror hanging on the wall and studied his reflection. The years had taken a toll, etching fine lines into the skin around his eyes and across his forehead.

He stroked his clean-shaven face. He'd shaved off his ever-present beard the day he'd "died." Maggie had always complained about his stubble. Matter of fact, toward the end of their time together, she'd complained about a lot. His hours at work, his hours away from home. His apparent lack of interest in his family.

What she never knew was that every hour spent away from his family was an hour spent trying to make the world a safer place for their daughter.

He reached into his duffel and extracted the small frame he'd taken before he'd left home for the last time. Maggie and a six-month-old Jordan grinned back from the silver frame.

What would Maggie say if she could see him now?

He glanced again at the mirror and then at the room. She'd probably love it here. He mentally berated himself, then tucked the frame between the mattress and box spring. Truth was, he had no idea of what Maggie would or wouldn't love at this stage of her life.

He'd heard rumors she'd become a hermit of sorts back in Seattle. The only comfort there was that even though Will had shown up in person to investigate the disappearance of their daughter, chances were, Maggie had not.

Will wondered exactly what Maggie had been told and what she believed. Did she accept the Royal Cielo Police's conclusion that Jordan had run away, or did her mother's intuition nag at her, warning her something far more sinister had taken place?

Will caught himself, shoving all thoughts of Maggie out of his brain.

Her thoughts weren't any of his business. He'd lost the right to think about her, to care about her, to love her, the day he'd walked away and never looked back. Check that, he should say the day he'd blown up and never looked back.

Hell of a choice for a man to make.

Desert your family and leave them grieving, or stay alive and risk their lives.

"Headed to the bunker?" Rick's deep voice sliced through Will's thoughts like a machete through a length of silk ribbon.

Will looked up to where Rick leaned against the door-jamb, a leather-bound book tucked beneath his arm, and nodded. "Can't take another minute in the loveliness of the accommodations."

Rick tossed back his head and laughed. "A bit different from the old days, isn't it?"

"You say that like we're ancient."

Rick's dark brows arched. "We *are* ancient."

The comfortable exchange renewed Will's hope and his determination. He and Rick had been through a lot over the years, and they'd always succeeded at whatever they put their minds to. This mission would be no different.

It couldn't be.

Failure wasn't an option.

"Were you headed downstairs?" Will asked.

Rick nodded. "I wanted to talk to you first."

Julian had already set their local investigation into motion. He'd set up the war room according to Will's instructions and he'd put word out to local informants that they would be looking—and paying—for information.

Kyle, Lily, and Julian had divided up the list of the Cielo's various points of departure in the hopes of finding someone who had seen Jordan. Will and Rick were headed out to pay a visit to the Royal Police Commissioner Dunkley.

"Are you afraid I won't remember how to run the show?" Will made a show of unpacking his duffel bag.

"Not likely." Rick moved next to him, dropping the book he carried on the bed. Will nodded toward the object, not giving voice to the question in his mind.

"I know you've already seen a recent photo of Jordan, but I thought you might want to see what you've missed. Maybe this will help you understand her a bit more."

"Not necessary." Will gave the book a shove, knowing instantly what his friend and partner had done.

"Understanding the body is step one in bringing her home, isn't that what we always say?"

Will breathed in slowly through his nose, working to contain his emotions, emotions he'd kept locked inside for so many years he'd forgotten they existed.

Anger. Resentment. Loss. Acceptance.

"She's not a body, Rick. She's my daughter."

Rick patted the album. "Then get to know her." He turned for the door. "Maggie's in there, too."

"No."

Will spoke the word so sharply Rick hesitated momentarily. "She's on the island, Will. Julian got word of her passing through customs earlier today."

Maggie.

On the island.

So she hadn't stayed in Seattle after all. For some reason, the thought she'd rushed to Cielo in search of their daughter made Will happy—and proud.

Just the same, there was no reason for either Jordan or Maggie to know Will was involved in the investigation.

"I'll stay in the shadows." Will hoisted the book from the bed, thrusting it toward Rick. "They'll never know I was here."

Rick clasped a hand on Will's shoulder, concern firing in his gaze. "Do you honestly believe that?"

Will said nothing, never breaking eye contact.

"Look at the photos, Will." Rick dropped his hand from Will's shoulder and headed back out into the hallway.

Will lowered his focus to the book in his hands. "Why?" Why would his friend have saved photos, clippings, whatever lay inside?

Rick blew out a breath before he answered. "Trust me. I know what it's like to have nothing."

Will grimaced, flashing back on the day Rick's young wife went missing during a sailing trip. In one afternoon, Rick's life had shifted, the future he'd planned with Janine had evaporated into thin air in the aftermath of a summer thunderstorm.

"I'm sorry," Will said. "I don't want to look at these."

Rick narrowed his eyes, the lines around his mouth growing tight. "I could never understand how you lived all these years without a call, without driving by their house. You were the one who died, my friend. Not them."

Will heard the accusation buried in his friend's words. Rick had never voiced his disappointment in

Will's inaction, but Will knew it was there, hanging between them.

"It's too painful to see them."

"Trust me." The years of pain and loss, wondering and searching, washed across Rick's features. "It's too painful not to."

Will stood motionless for several long moments after Rick walked away. He'd wondered every moment of every day how his wife and daughter were. Where they were. What they were doing. What they looked like. Who they loved.

But yet, he'd taken no action.

Rick was right. How had he gone all these years without looking? Without contact?

Maybe he was a coward. Or maybe staying away was the bravest thing he'd ever done in his life.

Will hoisted the book from the bed, opened the night-stand drawer and shoved the unwanted glimpse of the life he'd left behind out of sight.

If he opened the pages on the life he'd missed out on, how would he concentrate on the life he had? The life that required him to remain unemotional? Objective?

Right now he needed to focus on one thing, and one thing only. His mission: finding Jordan Connor and returning her to her mother alive.

If Will were smart, he'd convince himself Jordan was an anonymous seventeen-year-old who'd gotten herself into trouble during senior week. He'd convince himself he had no emotional ties to the case.

But even Will knew he wasn't that smart, no matter how hard he tried to believe otherwise.

CHAPTER FOUR

Body Clock: 34:55

"**M**ack Connor," Will introduced himself as he shook Police Commissioner Dunkley's hand.

He'd decided two things on the way to the police station.

One, leave Rick in the car as lookout and two, operate under the name by which Montoya had known him.

If the drug lord was on the island, why not get word to him as quickly as possible? The sooner Will and the team flushed the man out of hiding, the sooner they'd find Jordan.

Commissioner Dunkley looked unsure about Will's sudden visit. "And your interest in the case?"

"A private investigator from Seattle," Will answered. "And Jordan Connor's uncle."

"Mrs. Connor did not mention a brother when I met with her earlier."

"On her late husband's side." Will made a show of shaking his head. "I'm afraid we're a bit estranged."

Dunkley rocked back in his chair and pursed his lips. "I find myself wondering how you found out about your niece's disappearance so quickly."

"Media back home jumped all over the story," Will improvised quickly. "Local girl goes missing during her senior week trip." He made a snapping noise with his mouth. "Nothing they love more, unfortunately."

"Vultures," Dunkley said with a shake of his head.

"Exactly. Anyway, I wouldn't be able to sleep at night if I hadn't come here myself to check things out."

"We found no signs of struggle, Mr. Connor. And the young lady left a note detailing her plans to run away. I understand your concern, but there's truly nothing for you to check out."

Will frowned, doing his best to look sympathetic and intent. "I understand Miss Connor left her passport behind." He furrowed his brow. "Do you find that odd for someone running away?"

"Not if she went by boat. A person can island-hop for months and never need a passport, especially if she's with a local."

"I'd imagine so." Will's brain worked overtime. The team had the local ports covered, but Will needed to get his hands on the investigative notes.

He'd been called a control freak many times over the years on many cases, but he was very good at what he did for that reason. Will Connor left no stone unturned, and this time would be no different.

"Would it be possible for me to take a quick peek at the case file?" he asked.

Dunkley licked his lips.

Will zeroed in on the nervous move instantly.

Until that moment, the police commissioner had come across as nothing but straightforward, but his nonverbal slip painted a completely different picture.

The man was hiding something.

The commissioner made a show of frowning and shaking his head. "I'm afraid that file's already been archived." He met Will's stare, his focus unwavering. "I can have it pulled for you, but it won't be ready until tomorrow."

"Fair enough," Will said, pushing to his feet and extending his hand. "Thank you for your time.

I'll stop back tomorrow. Same time?"

"Perfect."

Dunkley's phone rang and Will stepped toward the hallway. "I'll see myself out." Dunkley nodded as Will pulled the office door shut behind him.

He had the distinct feeling the only way he'd get his hands on Jordan's case file would be to take it himself. To do so, he had to familiarize himself with the layout of the building quickly.

Will smiled at Dunkley's administrative assistant. "Could you point me in the direction of the men's room?"

"Of course." The young woman answered without looking up from her computer screen, tucking a strand of thick brown hair behind one ear as she frowned at whatever it was she was working on.

"Down this hall and around the corner. If the door's locked, just yell and I'll open it for you." She patted the top of her desk and looked up long enough to give Will a smile. "I'm the keeper of the keys."

"Many thanks." Will headed down the hall armed with not only the location of the restroom but also the location of the office keys. He'd no sooner begun his mental inventory of the precinct layout when someone entered from outside.

"Commissioner Dunkley, please."

The woman's voice wrapped its fingers around Will's heart and squeezed, riveting him to the spot. He pressed himself against an alcove and strained to see, trying for a glimpse of her. For a glimpse of his past.

Rick's information had obviously been correct.

Maggie had not only landed on the island, but she'd landed smack in the middle of Will's investigation.

Dunkley had said she'd been to the office earlier that day, so why was she back now?

Will held his ground, safely out of sight, listening. Not only could he hear Maggie's conversation with the assistant, but he could also pick up snippets of Dunkley's phone conversation.

Grateful for the building's shoddy construction, Will settled into the alcove, intent on finding out exactly what Maggie was up to.

Rick would have to sit tight out in the parking lot.

For now, Will wasn't going anywhere.

MAGGIE PACED the small waiting area just outside Commissioner Dunkley's office, her impatience simmering to a boil.

Dunkley might not be happy about her visit, but if he'd get off the damned phone and listen to her, he might be surprised at what she had to say.

Unless he already knew about the witness. Maybe the investigator hadn't been the only person to make light of Sonny's story.

She shook her head, mentally chastising herself.

She needed to go into Dunkley's office with an open mind. She needed the man's support if she wanted the investigation into Jordan's disappearance reopened. And, she needed him to go with her to meet Sonny.

Dunkley's voice filtered through the closed door, his words unintelligible, nothing more than a low drone. She glanced at her watch. A solid ten minutes had passed since his assistant had notified the man of Maggie's arrival.

Enough was enough.

She hit the door at a full stride, twisting open the knob and flinging the door open. Dunkley's eyes grew wide, and his lips quirked with amusement.

"I'll have to call you back," he said into the phone. Then to Maggie, "Mrs. Connor. Thanks so much for waiting." He gestured to a chair. "I understand you have some new information?"

"I do." Maggie chose to stand instead of sitting, her every nerve ending humming, anticipating Dunkley's reaction. "I was approached by someone who saw Jordan abducted."

The commissioner blinked. "Abducted?"

Maggie nodded. "By two men. I spoke with the witness, who, by the way, has already told his story to one of your responding officers."

"Ah." Dunkley folded his hands behind his head and rocked back in his chair. "I was afraid of this."

Maggie's nervous anticipation morphed into dread. "Of what?"

"Con artists," he answered. "They're going to come at you from all sides once word hits that you're on Cielo."

Con artists? She shook her head, quite certain Dunkley was mistaken. "This man was no con artist. I believe him."

"That, Mrs. Connor, is why we call them con artists. They're very good at what they do."

"No." Maggie began to pace in a tight pattern, Will's ring sitting heavy in the pocket of her jeans. "This man said he gave a statement to your officer. You're not listening to me. He's not making this up."

Dunkley pushed out of his chair and away from his desk, moving toward Maggie. She stilled, focusing on his eyes, his words.

"Informants expect to get paid, Mrs. Connor. He no doubt thought he could make up this story about an...abduction...to get money. My officers would have seen him for what he is."

"A con artist," she finished the thought for him.

Dunkley nodded and touched her arm lightly. "I'm

sorry."

"Well, that con artist found my—" Maggie caught herself, taking note of the way something shifted in Dunkley's expression.

His smug demeanor slipped for a moment, and if she wasn't mistaken, he looked eager...or anxious... about whatever it was her witness had found.

"Well?" He gestured for her to hurry up.

"He found me with no problem," Maggie improvised, suddenly deciding Dunkley didn't need to know about Will's wedding band.

Dunkley blew out an exasperated breath. "Most con artists are very good at finding their targets, Mrs. Connor. You, unfortunately, are the hottest target in town right now. You can expect plenty more to find you."

He moved away from her and Maggie found herself grateful for the space between them. A shiver inexplicably traced its way up her spine.

"What was your con artist's name?" Dunkley asked.

She thought momentarily about not answering, but then decided the information couldn't hurt. If anything, perhaps a name would add credibility.

"Sonny," she answered.

Dunkley's chortle started low and deep, building to full-out laughter.

He held up a hand. "Forgive me, but Sonny is notorious around here. He's probably back at your hotel robbing you blind while you run over here to tell me what he said. As a matter of fact—" he picked up the intercom and spoke softly into the receiver giving orders to have someone check her hotel "—I'd put money on it."

Great.

She stood her ground for a moment, then decided to tell Dunkley about the note. "He wants me to meet him at six."

"Tonight?" The man's features twisted in disbelief. "I would imagine you are much smarter than that. Yes?"

Silence beat between them for a brief moment.

"No," Maggie answered. "Actually, I had every intention of going to the meeting location. I was hoping you or one of your officers would go with me."

Dunkley made a tsking noise. "Nothing good will come out of this meeting. Trust me. If anything, he'll ask you for money with the promise of information he doesn't have."

Maggie pressed her fingertips to her pocket, tracing the edge of the ring. What Dunkley didn't know was that Sonny did have information. He'd had Will's ring and he'd seen Jordan abducted.

Yet, she couldn't bring herself to tell Dunkley.

Suddenly, she didn't trust the man.

"If that's all, Mrs. Connor, I do have other business to attend to. Do I have your assurance you'll be returning to your hotel and not to this meeting with Sonny?"

Maggie took a backward step toward the door, nodding, when in fact, she had no intention of returning to her hotel until she'd met Sonny.

"Why can't you send someone with me? What if

the man is telling the truth?"

"Mrs. Connor, forgive my vulgarity, but Sonny wouldn't know the truth if it bit him on the—"

Maggie held up her hand to cut him short. "I would think you'd want to pursue any lead we receive."

He pursed his lips and shook his head. "Your daughter's case is closed, Mrs. Connor, and my men have far better ways to spend their evenings." He returned to his desk and reached for the phone, making her dismissal quite evident. "Is there anything else?"

"Yes." Maggie stepped toward Dunkley's desk, palm outstretched. "My daughter's case file. If this case is closed, you obviously have no use for it."

Dunkley sat back against his chair, studying her before he spoke. "You Americans must think our case files are full of magic. Your brother-in-law was here a few moments ago asking for the same thing," he said, looking smug.

Brother-in-law?

"I don't have a brother-in-law, Commissioner." Maggie frowned. "Perhaps I'm not the only one who's become a target for con artists."

Dunkley's features fell.

"Perhaps—" Maggie stepped close, leaning over the desk and forcing a smile "—someone out there knows something, and they want the case file to make sure you don't figure out what really happened to my daughter."

Dunkley blew out a frustrated breath. "I'll have an officer track down Sonny, but you—" he pointed at her "—go directly back to your hotel. I'll be in touch."

But as Maggie headed out of the police precinct and back toward her car, she held no plans of following Dunkley's instructions.

Who knew when he'd get around to having Sonny questioned, and if someone else was looking for information on Jordan's disappearance, Maggie wasn't about to sit back and wait.

If there was information or evidence out there that had been missed, Maggie intended to find it before someone else could get to it first and make it disappear.

WILL PRESSED back against the darkened alcove and studied the woman as she raced out of Dunkley's office. The way she moved, the way she walked, the way she brushed her hair off her forehead in apparent frustration.

Maggie.

A weight pressed down on his chest. Seventeen years were gone in a blink of an eye. Seventeen years of not knowing, of pretending not to care, of working to forget her face, her lips, her eyes.

All Will's efforts to deny his past were gone with one brief glimpse of the woman he'd loved since he'd met her at a high-school dance.

He followed her steps just far enough to see her slip into a waiting taxi.

He'd had only a glimpse of the way the years had softened her face, saddened her eyes, but what he had seen reached deep inside him and tugged.

The cab pulled out of the parking lot, raising a

cloud of dust as it sped away.

Will hurried toward his car, sliding into the passenger seat, working to fight off the way the shock of seeing Maggie had slowed his movements.

Rick sat waiting, key in the ignition. "You okay?"

Will merely nodded. "Looks like Julian's info was right."

"Did she see Dunkley?"

Will nodded and straightened against the back of the seat. "She's been contacted by someone," he explained. "Someone who claims he saw Jordan. Dunkley's not buying it."

"Dunkley doesn't want to buy it."

"Precisely. The question is, why not?"

"Maybe he's in Montoya's pocket?"

"Could be." Will shrugged. "I wouldn't put it past Montoya to take on the Caribbean heroin trade, but how did he manage to stay off our radar for so long?"

Will realized the idiocy of his question even as he spoke the words.

Rick did nothing more than raise a brow. "Maybe Montoya and you aren't so different after all."

Will refocused on the empty spot where the cab had been. "The person who contacted her asked her to meet him at six tonight."

"She wouldn't be stupid enough to go alone, would she?" Rick asked.

"What do you think?" Protectiveness flared to life deep in Will's gut.

"You tell me. She's your wife."

"*Was* my wife," Will said flatly. He tipped his

chin toward the Commissioner's office. "She wanted someone to go with her. Dunkley told her to ignore the meet. Told her she's a target for crackpots and he'd follow up on the lead."

"Maybe I should give Dunkley more credit than I have."

"Not likely."

Will drew in a steadying breath as Rick cranked on the ignition and shifted the car into First.

"Safe following distance?" Will asked.

"Should be just about perfect," Rick said as he pulled out of the drive, headed in the same direction as Maggie's cab, the vehicle's taillights still visible down the long stretch of road ahead.

CHAPTER FIVE

Body Clock: 36:45

The cab let Maggie out next to a busy downtown street market. She took in her surroundings, noting the shadows cast by the brightly colored shops and the angle of the late-day sun.

Faces.

She should be studying faces. But for what? For whom?

She launched herself into motion, studying the scribbled note in her hand. The cab driver had told her she'd need to walk one half block to her destination. She checked the time. Five forty-five. Her defense training urged her to arrive ahead of Sonny to avoid making herself vulnerable.

She stopped, looking again over one shoulder and then the other, the small hairs at the base of her neck prickling to attention. A sense of foreboding flooded her senses.

What if Commissioner Dunkley was right? What if she had no business being here? What if meeting Sonny was a terrible mistake and he was nothing more than a common thief out to snatch her wallet and run?

But she knew differently. He'd had Jordan's ring.

But what if he'd been involved? What if Sonny had been more than an innocent witness?

Her instincts told her to trust the man, but what if her instincts were wrong?

Maggie pressed a palm against a store's wall, drawing in a slow breath through her nose, holding it for four counts, before blowing out the air through her mouth.

Calm yourself, Maggie. Calm yourself.

She looked across the street, catching her reflection and that of the old building she leaned against in the window of a modern office building.

The contrast of old and new sharpened her senses, a tangible reminder of just how far she'd come.

The old Maggie would be sitting at home in Seattle wringing her hands and pacing the floors with worry. The new Maggie was here, in Isle de Cielo, doing what the police refused to do.

She was looking for her daughter.

"Mrs. Connor."

The sound of her name was nothing more than a whisper among the myriad voices surrounding her. She pushed away from the wall, smoothing her palms over her tunic top and the front of her capris. She saw no one. No one she recognized as Sonny.

Had the man set her up?

"Mrs. Connor." The voice sounded again, this time next to her right ear.

Maggie spun, reflexively raising her arms in front of her face, expecting a mugging, an attack, something.

She was greeted instead by Sonny's face, grinning out at her from beneath a large, wide-brimmed hat.

Maggie blinked.

The man before her in no way resembled the man with whom she'd spoken on the beach.

"You look—"

"Civilized," Sonny answered before Maggie could finish her thought. He ran a hand down the front of his white linen suit and whistled. "I clean up well, don't I?" Linking his arm through Maggie's, he steered her away from the building. "Let's walk, shall we?"

"Do you know where my daughter—"

Sonny pressed a finger to Maggie's lips, chilling her with the overly familiar gesture. "No talking. Not yet. The walls have ears."

Maggie nodded, swallowing down the tangle of fear and anxiety in her throat.

She followed Sonny's lead, turning into a small alleyway that opened into a garden. He pointed to a wrought-iron bench and Maggie sat, clasping and unclasping her hands.

Sonny stood before her, frowning down at her hands. "You have no need to fear me, Mrs. Connor."

"Commissioner Dunkley said the exact opposite." Maggie pressed her palms to her knees, working to hide her nerves.

Sonny removed his hat and ran a hand over his head, grinning. "I'm afraid you would be wise to fear the good commissioner more than anyone."

Maggie straightened. "Why?"

Sonny leaned close, dropping his voice low. "Because Commissioner Dunkley knows exactly what happened to your daughter, and he'll do whatever he has to do to make sure you don't find out."

WILL FILLED Rick in on his exchange with Dunkley as they tailed Maggie's cab into Newmarket. "And you honestly believe this guy will give you the case file?" Rick asked.

Will shook his head. "Not without cleaning it up first."

"So?"

"So, we take it." Will patted the dashboard.

"Tonight?"

"The sooner the better."

They sat in silence for a few moments before Will decided to come fully clean. "I gave Dunkley my real name."

"Mack Connor?" Rick shot him a glare, then refocused on the road. He opened his mouth, as if ready to tell Will he had a death wish, but then said nothing. Nothing at all.

"I want Montoya," Will said flatly, aware of his pulse beating in his ears.

"And apparently, the feeling's mutual." Rick tipped his chin toward the road ahead. "There they go. I'll close the gap."

The small cab took a turn down the main shopping street, moving slowly through the throng of pedestrians—tourists and locals—who had apparently decided the mild evening was perfect for shopping.

Rick hung back as the cab slowed to a stop and Maggie climbed out of the back. As the cab pulled away, she searched those around her, a mix of fear and stubbornness on her face.

"She looks good," Rick said. "Strong." And she did.

Her long blond hair fell into soft waves, more carefree than Will remembered, although that might have been the island's influence. Her black tunic-style T-shirt stopped short of her hips, hugging the cropped white jeans she wore as though she hadn't aged a day during the years Will had been gone.

A man edged to her side, and Maggie seemed completely unaware. He wore a large hat and a white suit, and he moved with purpose, making it obvious to anyone watching that Maggie was his intended target.

Will reached for the door handle, protectiveness surging through him.

"Wait," Rick cautioned. "We may need this guy. Don't run him off just yet."

They crawled along behind the unlikely pair as they made their way down the sidewalk, the man's arm linked through Maggie's.

"I'm not liking this," Will growled beneath his breath.

"Don't worry. By the looks of things, neither is she."

Rick pressed on the brake, bringing the car to a full stop the moment Maggie and her companion turned down a narrow alleyway.

"Go."

Will was already on the move, one foot planted on the street. He gave the car door a shove behind him as he stepped out, cutting diagonally through the steady stream of tourists, never taking his eyes from the alley.

He slowed at the corner, stealing a glance to locate where Maggie and the man had gone. He spotted them instantly.

She sat on a bench backing the alley, facing a lush, tropical garden. The man paced in front of her, hands working as if he struggled to make a point, to tell her something.

Will forced himself to focus on the man and not on Maggie, though his eyes continued to stray back to the gentle curve of her cheek, the slender profile of her jaw and neck, the way a sudden breeze lifted a strand of her hair across her face.

He followed the touch of her fingers, tucking the hair behind her ear as he'd seen her do countless times before.

He'd been crazy to leave her alone so long ago. How could he have done it? How could he have walked away from his wife? His child? His life?

A small white car whizzed past him, taking the corner on two wheels.

The driver's profile suggested youth, and Will grimaced. Just what he didn't need. Some kid getting his jollies by driving down a back alley when Will was trying to run surveillance.

When the car jerked to stop mere feet from where Maggie sat, an altogether different emotion overtook Will.

Foreboding.

The driver bailed from the car, taking off in a sprint toward the other side of the alley.

Maggie and the man in the suit continued their heated exchange, apparently unaware of the car's arrival and the driver's hasty departure.

Will, however, was already in motion, moving quickly and stealthily along the alley wall, headed straight for the car.

He knew what he was going to see in the split second before he hit his knees to peer beneath the car.

The bomb looked eerily similar to the device that had forever changed his life...and Maggie's.

Will launched himself into motion, heading for Maggie in a full-out sprint. Cover be damned. Potential witness be damned.

A bomb like that was meant to do only one thing, and he wasn't about to let Maggie become a victim today.

"ARE YOU trying to tell me Commissioner Dunkley is involved in Jordan's disappearance?" Maggie asked.

Sonny shook his head. "Not involved. Just looking the other way."

"Why?"

The small man rubbed his thumb and fingertips together the way people do to indicate money. "We are not a rich country, and I'm afraid not even the commissioner is above the law."

"But surely he wouldn't hide a young woman's abduction?"

"It wouldn't be the first time."

"What are you saying?"

"I'm saying this is not the first time a young woman has vanished during her holiday."

"And the others?"

He shrugged. "Alive and working, but not anywhere a mother would want them to be."

"Slavery?"

"Such a harsh word."

"But accurate?"

"Yes, Mrs. Connor. Very accurate."

Bile clawed at the back of Maggie's throat. Jordan. Human trafficking. Slave labor...or worse. "Do you know for a fact this is what's happened to Jordan?"

He narrowed his eyes, as if he needed more than a question to prod his memory bank.

"I'll pay you." Maggie winced at the pathetic tone of her voice.

It was amazing how quickly all those years of safety training flew out the window when it was a matter of rescuing your daughter from a living hell.

"Whatever you want," she moved to stand, but Sonny motioned for her to stay seated, "I'll pay you."

"I can only guess. I do not know for certain."

Now it was Maggie's turn to narrow her eyes. "Why not?"

"The men I saw with her." He squinted. "One I know. One I do not know."

"The one you know." This time she stood, whether he wanted her to or not. "Tell me his name. Please. I'll pay you whatever price you require. Please tell me."

"Doc."

Hope swirled to life inside her.

"This Doc, does he live on the island?"

Sonny shook his head. "Born and raised here, but Cielo isn't the place to be for his business."

"People." Maggie shuddered as she said the word.

"People." He nodded. "He operates out of the Dominican Republic."

"Is that where he takes the girls?"

Jordan, she screamed inside her head. *Please, not Jordan.*

But before Sonny could give her an answer, pounding footsteps sounded loudly from behind them.

She moved to turn, to see what was happening, but the look on Sonny's face froze her in midmotion. His eyes had gone huge, full of fear.

"Damn," he murmured under his breath as he turned to run.

An explosion sounded. Sharp. Deafening. Rattling Maggie to her very core. Someone slammed her down to the unforgiving ground, entangling her in a mess of arms and legs.

She struggled to roll away, struggled to free herself, to run, to hide, to survive.

Smells assaulted her senses. Burning rubber. Smoke. The garden's tropical blooms.

And something else. Another scent toyed with her, teasing at her memory, even as she struggled to free

KATHLEEN LONG

herself from her attacker.

"Don't move. Let me make sure you're not hurt."

And then it hit her. The voice. The clean smell of the soap he'd insisted on using for as long as she'd known him. The feel of her body, safely enfolded inside his strong arms.

Will.

Maggie's body went slack, her heart exploded in her chest. She pushed against him, her gaze finding his, sudden tears clouding her vision.

His face was older than she remembered, the features more sharply drawn.

Lines bracketed his brown eyes, and a vertical crease marred his forehead, but his dark hair fell into the same cowlick she'd always remembered. After his death, she'd imagined the remembered feel of his hair beneath her fingers, time after time, year after year.

A trickle of blood slid down his cheek toward the line of his jaw. Maggie reached for him, brushing away the blood, touching the wound, amazed at the feel of his skin beneath her fingertip.

His warm, alive, living, breathing skin.

"Will?"

He nodded.

Her heart sank and soared in the same beat.

Being in Will's arms could only mean one thing.

She was dead.

And if she were dead, she'd failed Jordan, leaving her alone just when Jordan needed her most.

"Will?" she asked again.

"Right here," he answered. "I've got you."

I've got you.

If only.

Maggie's vision swam. Then her world turned black.

A SCRAPING NOISE woke Jordan from a dreamless sleep. Much as she'd tried to stay awake, tried to search her underground prison for a way out, hunger and thirst had won out and she'd fallen asleep, backed into a corner, head slumped to one side.

"Not happy with the accommodations?" Jaime asked.

Emotional pain sliced through her at the sound of his voice. She rubbed her stiff neck and forced her eyes open, shocked again by the lack of life in the look that met hers.

Jaime's brown eyes were dead. A shaft of sunlight streamed through the hole in the ceiling, lighting his face, illuminating nothing but his lack of emotion. Lack of heart. Lack of almost everything human.

The man was dead inside.

How had she not seen that before?

He reached for her, gripping her arm roughly and forcing her to her feet. "The good doctor had to make another house call, so I'll be giving you your shot tonight."

"Shot?" She forced the word through an impossibly parched throat. "Why are you doing this to me?"

"The question, dear Jordan—" he shoved her toward the wooden slab "—is why I didn't do this sooner. The answer would be timing."

A grin so evil it sent ice sliding through Jordan's veins spread wide across Jaime's face. "It's all about timing. You'd understand that if you were a bit more experienced."

"You said you loved me." She cringed at the choked sound of her voice.

"And you believed me." He laughed. "So predictable, and a bit sad, don't you think?"

Pain ripped through her insides—physical, emotional, raw—a mix of heartbreak and panic.

How could she have been so stupid?

"Please, can't I have some water?" she asked.

Jamie gave her a push and she fell against the wooden bed, the rough edge of the slab cutting into her bare legs. "Now why would I give you water?"

"You're going to let me die here, aren't you?"

He flipped the top off a syringe and wrapped his fingers around her upper arm. Jordan thought about struggling, thought about fighting, but she knew better. She had nowhere to go in this dank, dark hole. And if she ever wanted to figure a way out, she had to save her strength for a time when Jaime wasn't there. For the minutes after the shot wore off and before he returned the next time.

Jaime stabbed the needle into her upper arm and Jordan winced. As he depressed the plunger, he spoke, amusement dripping from his words. "Whether or not you die down here depends on one person only. Your father."

"My father's dead," Jordan answered, the statement never failing to make her heart ache, no matter how many times she'd uttered the words before.

Jaime made a snapping noise with his mouth. "That's where you're wrong. Your father is very much alive. Matter of fact, I happen to know he's here in Cielo."

What? Was Jaime insane?

"My father died in a car explosion seventeen years ago, when I was just a baby."

"So he wanted you to think." Jaime shook his head and frowned. "Can you imagine doing something so heartless to your family?"

Darkness began to overtake Jordan's sight, spreading like a black fog across her field of vision.

Jaime stood, moving across the room, but try as she might, Jordan couldn't see what he was doing. If only she could stay conscious long enough to see how he came and went from the underground prison.

"Your father's been alive all these years," Jaime said, his voice fading. "He just didn't want to be with you. Dream about that, sweet Jordan."

Jaime's words tore at Jordan's soul.

Could her father be alive?

Jordan had spent her entire life praying for her father's return, even though she knew it wasn't possible. She'd built him up to be a hero in her mind. A man among men.

Yet, what kind of father would let his family believe him dead? Certainly not the father Jordan had fabricated in her thoughts and dreams.

As darkness overtook the light, Jordan realized that if her father was alive, he could never measure up to the man she'd created in her mind. The man she'd imagined would never leave his family alone and grieving. He was a hero—a hero who would find her, save her, make Jaime pay for what he'd done.

But if Jaime's words were true, her father was any-thing but a hero.

Jaime had said her father was in Cielo. But why? To find her? Or to leave her just as he'd done before?

Only this time, if her father left Jordan, he'd be leaving her to die.

CHAPTER SIX

Body Clock: 39:05

Maggie blinked her eyes open, aware of a sharp pain along the side of her face. She reached for her cheek, wincing when her fingertips grazed an area of abrasion and swelling.

She did her best to focus on her surroundings, trying to recognize the brightly patterned green curtains swaying in the breeze, the white plaster walls, the ornate bed frame.

Where was she?

And what had happened?

The memories came back in flashes, glimpses of faces and sounds and smells.

Damn, Sonny had said just seconds before the explosion. The air had smelled burned, metallic, and then there'd been someone else.

Will.

Maggie sat straight up in bed with a gasp.

Will had saved her.

She looked around the room again. Was this Heaven?

The room's lone door opened and Will appeared, like a vision from her dreams.

"Will?" The name sounded odd on her lips, it had been so long since she'd spoken it out loud. Her husband had been a man of such determination that she'd started calling him Will instead of Mack not long after their marriage.

Where there was a Will, there was a way.

"Will?" she repeated. "Is that you?"

The man nodded. Maggie drank in the sight of him, the strong body, the muscled shoulders and arms, the clean-shaven face—a bit leaner than she remembered, the brown eyes more the color of whiskey than chocolate. Just like Jordan's.

Tears stung her eyes. "Where am I?"

"A safe house," he answered, taking a tentative step closer.

"Am I dead?"

"Close," he said. "But not quite."

"Am I in limbo?"

"You might say that." Her question caused him to smile. Maggie's heart caught. Oh, how she'd missed his smile.

Will moved to sit beside her on the bed. The mattress sagged with his weight and Maggie reached for him, pressing the palm of her hand to his cheek even as her tears spilled over her lashes.

"We're on Isle de Cielo." He placed his hand over

hers, covering her fingers with his. "Do you remember that?"

"Jordan," Maggie said softly.

"Jordan," Will repeated. "I followed you from Dunkley's office."

"You were the brother-in-law he mentioned?"

Will nodded. "There was a bomb. We think it was meant for the man you were with."

"What happened to him?" Maggie flashed again on Sonny's expression just before the blast.

"He managed to get away."

"And the police?"

Will squinted momentarily. "We took you out of there before they could respond. Until we know who was behind this, the safest place for you is right here."

"And here is a safe house?" she asked, suddenly drained of all emotion and energy.

Will nodded.

Myriad thoughts swirled through Maggie's mind. Jordan. Cielo. Dunkley. Bomb. Sonny. Will.

This was all so incredibly surreal, as if she'd stepped into some sort of dream world. But Will...

How could this be?

"You're not dead?" she asked, her past flashing through her mind like pictures on a movie screen. The years alone without Will.

The tears.

The grief.

The nights spent cradling his pillow to her chest.

The visceral pain that had never gone away, no matter how many times some well-meaning acquaintance had told her time healed all wounds.

Time had healed nothing.

"I'm not dead," he answered, tightening his grip on her hand.

But Maggie slid her hand free from his, free of the contact with his cheek. She pushed to her feet, launching herself toward the opposite side of the room.

Her head swam. Dizziness washed over her, but she ignored the sensation, focusing on Will's words, on his presence—his very alive, very real presence.

She spun on him, even as he closed the space between them.

Her slap connected with the same cheek she'd just caressed. The tears that stung her eyes now were anything but tears of joy.

"You son of a bitch."

"Fair enough." Will caught her wrist. "Now let me explain why I did what I did."

"You can't possibly explain what you did." Maggie tried to jerk free of his touch, but failed. If anything, Will's fingers wrapped more tightly around her wrist. "You're hurting me."

"I would never hurt—"

A bitter laugh spilled across Maggie's lips. "No, you'd never hurt me, would you, Will? You'd simply desert me."

"Maggie." Will grasped her shoulders, moving so quickly she found herself toe-to-toe with him. Too close. "I had no choice. I don't expect you to understand."

"Take. Your. Hands. Off. Me."

He did as she asked, breaking their contact, yet not moving. If anything, he leaned closer. She pressed back against the wall, willing her body to shrink as far away from him as possible.

"I did what I needed to do." His dark gaze narrowed, intensified.

Maggie couldn't believe her ears. "What? Abandon your family?"

"*Save* my family." He stressed the first word, hoisting his chin proudly.

"*Save* us?" Anger ripped through Maggie, tearing at her insides. "You *destroyed* us."

"No." Will shook his head. "I made the choice I had to make."

Maggie squeezed her eyes shut, her mind working frantically to accept the reality of her situation. Jordan was missing. Will was alive, and Maggie stood debating with him in the middle of some stranger's bedroom on a Caribbean island.

She blinked, working to keep her thoughts focused.

"There's always a second option." She pressed her lips together momentarily, meeting his intense stare, fighting not to lose herself in the heat of his dark gaze. "Maybe if you'd asked me, I would have given you a different option."

Will's features softened and Maggie's insides twisted. Their last several weeks together had been heated, angry. It had been so long since she'd seen a kind expression on his face that the sight of it now threatened to strip away every ounce of her resolve to hate him.

"Anything else would have cost you your life. Jordan's life."

"That wasn't your decision to make." She forced the words through a throat choked with emotion, shock and disbelief.

"I'm part of a covert group," he explained. "And I was closing in on one of the biggest heroin smugglers in the world. He threatened to kill you both. I died to save you."

Maggie's brain had snagged on his first sentence.

"Covert group?" She frowned, skeptical. "You and Rick organized trade shows, for crying out loud. Are you trying to tell me you're part of the CIA or something?"

"Or something," he answered. "The details aren't important now."

She patted her chest. "Maybe they're important to me. Your wife. Remember?"

"I need you to try to understand, Maggie. For Jordan's sake."

She shoved at his chest, pushing past him, needing space. Lots of space.

"No." She bit out the word, pointing a finger at his stubborn features. "Don't you dare play that card. What you did happened seventeen years ago. Don't think the current crisis excuses what you did to us back then."

"Maggie, I—"

She held up a hand as she paced, her moves erratic, like those of a wild woman. She didn't care.

"What did you think, Will? Did you think I'd roll over and say thank-you? Thank you for destroying our lives in order to save them?" She pulled back the hair she kept carefully layered to frame her face, to hide her scars.

Some sick satisfaction tugged at her insides when Will flinched.

She traced a fingertip along the angry scar, her very own personal souvenir of the day her husband died, as if the sudden, gaping void in her life hadn't been enough of a reminder.

"This is what fate handed me. I almost died trying to reach the scene of your accident." She let her fingertip stop just short of her temple. "Another inch and our daughter would have become an orphan that day."

She turned her back to him, but just as quickly spun back to face him, her anger boiling inside her, threatening to explode in a tirade of screaming and hitting and swearing.

Maggie held herself together, in control. She'd worked long and hard to master the ability to handle her reactions to every situation she might face.

She'd never dreamed, however, that she might someday face Will—alive.

"Just whose body was it I buried?" she asked.

Will's throat worked and for the briefest moment, the carefully erected wall that hid his every emotion faltered, showing a glimpse of remorse. At least, she'd like to think it was remorse.

"A cadaver," he answered. "From the university."

"Great." She shook her head and pushed away from the wall, crossing to the window, the sight of the picture-perfect scene outside turning her stomach. "Let the university know they owe me six thousand dollars in funeral expenses."

"Maggie…"

"No." She spun on him. "Don't you 'Maggie' me. Not ever again."

The door creaked open and Maggie turned just as Rick stepped into the room.

She laughed in disbelief. "I should have known. You two never could stand to be apart for more than fifteen minutes."

"Will made the choice he felt he had to make," Rick said, skipping past any sort of greeting.

Maggie realized he'd been listening from the other side of the door.

"And you? You went along with it, even as you sat by my side in the hospital listening to my tears? All part of your little covert operation?" She waved her hand dismissively.

Rick nodded, saying nothing.

"You knew about her accident?" Will asked as he shifted his focus to Rick.

"I couldn't tell you," Rick answered. "You'd have gone to her. It was for your own good."

"So now you get a little taste of the deception. Not so sweet, is it?" Maggie brushed past Will and Rick as she fled the room. "If you two will excuse me, I need to get as far away from you both as I can."

"What about Jordan?"

Rick's question fully captured Maggie's attention. Refocusing her thoughts.

Jordan.

"What do you know?" She pivoted on one heel, hope firing inside her.

Rick stepped past Maggie, pulling open a door set so smoothly into the wall, Maggie hadn't noticed its existence.

"The team's waiting to debrief," he said. "That's why I came for you both."

"Both?" Maggie's voice climbed an octave.

"We're in this together." Will reached for her, but she turned her back, saying nothing as Rick pointed down a set of stairs to the safe house's bunker.

WILL HESITATED, momentarily stunned by the depth of Maggie's anger. He had no reason to be surprised. No reason to have expected anything different.

He couldn't begin to imagine how he'd feel if their situations were reversed, even if what he'd done seventeen years earlier had been the correct call. The only call.

"The team's waiting." Rick dropped his voice low.

Will shifted his focus from the back of Maggie's head to Rick, knowing his old friend was right.

There wasn't time to focus on Maggie right now. He shouldn't. And he wouldn't.

"Let's go." He clasped a hand on Rick's shoulder, heading down the bunker steps.

As he hit the bottom of the stairs and stepped

into the war room, Will studied the satellite photos of the island, the charts, the diagrams the team had diligently prepared, and the expectant expression on each team member's face.

He'd become a master at compartmentalizing tasks and thoughts over the years. He stole a glance at Maggie as she dropped into an empty chair.

Why should emotions be any different?

Everyone was present but Lily, who'd had the farthest to travel in her investigation of island ports.

Will gestured to Maggie. "Maggie Connor. Jordan's mother. My wife." He pointed to each team member, introducing them. "Kyle Landenburg. Julian Harris. Silvia Hellman."

Then Will shoved all thoughts of Maggie into a tiny mental compartment and launched into the debriefing.

There was work to do.

"We've got to get a bead on Montoya. Either he's set up an operations base on Cielo, or he's got someone here. What have we got?"

Julian and Kyle both shook their heads, having uncovered no new information. Silvia, however, pushed away from the wall of computer screens, her expression solemn. Will knew instantly that whatever she was about to say couldn't be good.

"I found Montoya." She handed Will a black-and-white photograph. "I don't think he's our man." He stared down into the face that had forced his hand into leaving his family.

Diego Montoya.

In the photo, Montoya was most definitely dead, the victim of a close-range gunshot wound. "How do we know this isn't doctored?"

"Trust me." Silvia plucked a pile of printouts from the computer table. "It's not."

She handed the pile to Will, and he quickly flipped through the sheets. Altered hospital reports. Duplicate sets of death certificates. Photographs of gravesites.

"Isabel Montoya was killed one month before your 'death,'" Silvia explained. "She was caught in the cross-fire of the internal war that broke out in Montoya's organization as the result of you shutting down one of their distribution routes."

"So coming after my family wasn't business," Will said, staring again at Montoya's shattered face.

Silvia shook her gray head. "It was personal."

"Who took him out?" Will asked.

He crossed to the bulletin board and pinned the gruesome photo next to the old headshot of the drug lord.

Maggie winced and looked away.

"Suicide." Silvia's answer rocked Will straight through.

"Suicide?"

Montoya? Never.

The older woman nodded, no doubt reading the unspoken questions in Will's expression.

"Reeling with grief, disgraced by not being the one to kill you, and with his organization falling apart, he turned his gun on his thirteen-year-old son and then killed himself."

His thirteen-year-old son.

Bastard.

He flipped through the set of reports one more time. "So the cartel hid everything? He's been dead this entire time?"

"His suicide would have altered their status in the pecking order of the worldwide drug trade. It was better to have him simply disappear," she answered.

Maggie pushed to her feet and raced for the stairs, her thoughts apparently having followed the same path Will's had.

If Montoya had been dead for seventeen years, Will had stayed away from his family for no reason.

Yet if that argument were completely accurate, why would someone snatch Jordan now?

"Where are you going?" Will moved to follow Maggie, but Rick held up a hand, blocking his path. Will shot Rick a warning glare as Maggie called out her answer.

"I need some air."

Will shoved at Rick's arm, but met nothing but resistance. "It isn't safe for you out there," he called out. "Not anymore."

"What are you going to do, Will?" Maggie asked. "Jump in front of a bullet for me?"

"As a matter of fact—"

He pushed past Rick and headed for the steps. The other team members had shifted their focus away from Will out of respect.

Will raced up the steps, but Maggie was gone.

He felt Rick's presence behind him. "The team's waiting."

"Then let them wait."

Will hesitated at the threshold to the outside, momentarily mind-boggled that he'd walked out of a team meeting. So much for compartmentalization.

He followed Maggie, staying back out of her sight, watching as she headed for the main road, then hailed a passing taxicab.

He raced back to the house, grabbed the keys for one of the team cars and took off in a sprint. He cranked the ignition and pulled out recklessly, not caring if he drew unwanted attention.

His mind reeled with everything that had happened, and he was losing control.

He forced himself to breathe, to regain his trademark composure, and then he followed Maggie's cab until the driver deposited her at the front door to her hotel.

Will breathed a sigh of relief.

She'd be safe there, at least long enough for him to get back to the team, back to the search for Jordan.

Rick had been right.

The team was waiting.

Seeing Maggie again had made Will lose his focus and his control, something he couldn't afford to do.

Montoya was dead.

They'd been chasing a ghost.

So, who had taken Jordan? And why?

The team would have to start over from square one. Motivations. Enemies. Theories.

Will thought of Jordan, her photograph flashing through his mind.

Chasing a ghost.

He could only pray they weren't chasing two.

THE FIRST THING Maggie noticed when she walked into her hotel room was the gauze curtain billowing in the sea breeze. She'd locked the doors when she and Eileen had last been in the room. She was sure of it.

Her focus dropped to the room, or rather, what was left of the room. The bedspread and linens lay in a heap against the far wall, the mattress and box spring upended and gutted. The pillows had been shredded and the two drawers into which Maggie had unpacked her weekend bag had been dumped.

Bile clawed at the back of her throat, but Maggie bit it back.

Whoever had done this had obviously approached from the beach, breaking in through the French doors leading to the patio.

But who? And why? Sonny? Will said Sonny had gotten away from the explosion, but surely he'd been injured. He must have been.

If he hadn't done this, then who? And what had they been looking for?

She pressed her fingertips to the pocket of her jeans, tracing the hard outline of Will's ring.

Did someone else out there know about the ring? Know it represented the only piece of hard evidence to suggest Jordan had been abducted forcefully?

The flooring in the bathroom creaked and Maggie's

heart knotted in her chest.

Fool.

She'd been so consumed by her thoughts, she hadn't made sure the intruder was gone.

A shape moved in her peripheral vision, but before she could raise an arm defensively, scream, move, do anything, something crashed into her shoulder, sending her flying forward, face down on the hard floor.

As her head connected with the wooden frame of the bed, she forced her mind to focus on one thing only.

Survival.

CHAPTER SEVEN

Body Clock: 40:20

The team had reassembled after Will's return, each member knowing better than to mention their team leader's loss of control.

"I have one more thing on Montoya." Silvia's pale blue eyes shone brightly.

"Lit with information," Will always called the look. The woman would never make a great poker player. As soon as she had a good hand, her eyes would sparkle.

"Isabel Montoya's grave," she continued.

"What about it?" Will took another printout from her hands, staring down at the image of three elaborate tomb-stones. Father. Mother. Son.

"Diego Montoya placed a single white orchid on his wife's grave every Sunday in the weeks before his death." Her silver brows lifted. "The grave's vase sat empty after his suicide."

Will didn't have to ask what had happened next. He could see the orchid with his own eyes. He tapped a fingertip to the photo. "When was this taken?"

"Last week," she answered, blowing out a sigh. "On the seventeenth anniversary of Montoya's suicide, the first new orchid appeared. There has been a fresh orchid in the vase ever since."

"So either Montoya is back from the dead—" Will glanced at the gory photo of the man's face "—which is unlikely."

"Or someone else has decided to take over operations," Kyle said.

"Or come after me." Will patted his chest. "But why?"

"Revenge?" Julian offered.

"Why wait until now?" Will asked.

"Revenge is a dish best served cold." Rick lifted his brows.

The reinforced door to the bunker swung open, breaking the team's concentration. Lily had returned.

If the young agent had been walking on the beach or lounging at a poolside bar, she would have turned heads with her trim figure, curve-baring halter top and filmy gauze skirt. Instead, Will and the other agents focused on the fact she'd returned ahead of schedule.

"She's on the island." Her voice rang heavy with excitement as she handed her purse to Silvia. "They transported her by boat."

Silvia popped a tiny memory card out of the purse's buckle and slid it into one of the computers. She keyed in a command and a series of photos appeared on a full wall screen that slid out of the ceiling.

Lily walked toward the wall, talking excitedly. "This is the *King of the Sea*." She pointed to a large yacht, noting a second photo that showed the moniker emblazoned across the stern of the boat. "My witness puts a young woman matching Jordan's description on this boat at seven o'clock in the morning, leaving port."

She moved to the wall where a large map of Cielo hung, pointing first at a spot just south of Jordan's hotel and then at a point one-quarter of the way around the island, on the Atlantic side. "This is where I found the boat.

"The *King of the Sea* arrived here four hours later," she continued. "Two passengers came through the port entry office. Two men. One the right age to be our elusive Jaime, the other older, his face badly scarred."

Montoya's hired help, no doubt.

"And how many left the first port?" Rick asked.

"Three. One of them the young girl matching Jordan's description. Only here's the thing. She was apparently unconscious, her companion stated she'd had too much to drink and needed to sleep things off."

"How do we know she wasn't left behind on the boat?" Julian asked.

"The Royal Cielo Police were doing random searches that day. They have documentation on the King of the Sea being searched. Top to bottom." She wiped her hands together. "Clean."

Will crossed the room to the map, tracing his finger from the first port to the second. "So our best guess is that Jordan was left somewhere between these two points."

Lily nodded. "Either at a smaller port or private dock."

"Could be anywhere," Rick said.

Will smiled, hope suffusing through his body for the first time since Jordan had vanished. "But she's not *anywhere*." He plucked a black marker from the worktable and circled the lower section of the island. "She's here. Jordan is somewhere in this region. Now all we have to do is find her."

He pivoted on one heel. "And we have to find all of the registration information for that yacht."

Silvia, however, was already hard at work. "*King of the Sea*," she read from the screen. "Registered to a Ferdinand King. Resident of Isle de Cielo, West Indies."

"Ferdinand King." Will frowned. "Why is that name so—"

"King is known as a humanitarian," Julian answered. "He's known for making large cash gifts to local charities and maintains homes on Cielo, in the Dominican Republic, and in Switzerland."

"I see you've paid attention during your travels," Will said, proud of the young agent's knowledge.

Julian grimaced. "You won't like what I say next." He narrowed his gaze. "King is also suspected of operating the largest human-trafficking ring in the Caribbean."

Human trafficking.

Will's blood ran cold. Had Jordan been swept up into the horrific world of slave labor and sexual predators? But yet, her kidnapping hadn't been random.

We meet again. He glanced at the board and the faxed note that had launched their investigation.

With Montoya dead, where was the connection?

"King's mansion is an hour away by car," Lily continued. "I've already confirmed he's in residence."

"Excellent," Will answered. "Kyle, how quickly can you have the cars ready to leave—"

But when Will turned to face the senior operative, the faraway look on Kyle's face stopped Will in his tracks. The man knew something. Sensed something.

"Kyle?"

The signal on the local police scanner sounded, and Rick crossed the room, reading the display. When he turned back to face the group, his typically controlled expression was anything but.

"There's been a reported break-in and assault at Maggie's hotel. In a guest room."

Will's heart slammed against his ribs.

He should never have let her go in alone.

"I'll drive," Kyle said, already moving through the door as the team sprang into action.

PAIN AND PANIC closed in on Maggie, pushing from all sides. She could give up. Surrender. Stop fighting what felt like the inevitable, but then she'd never find Jordan.

And she'd never see Will again. As incomprehensible as the man's actions had been, Will's face flashed through her mind's eye now, right next to Jordan's. The two faces she refused never to see again.

Her attacker was on top of her, pinning her to the floor.

A sudden burst of determination exploded inside her.

She'd come to Cielo for a reason. To find Jordan and take her home. She had no intention of letting some two-bit thug take that away from her.

The man shifted on top of her, and her mind began to run through the awful possibilities of what he was about to do. She writhed beneath him, clawing at the floor, clinging to the frame of the bed, working to pull herself free.

"Where is it?" he asked, his voice parched and raspy, as if he'd gone days without liquid.

"What?" Maggie grunted the word and she fought, doing everything in her power to work her body free of the weight on top of her.

"The ring." This time when the man spoke, his voice rang clear and strong, sending a shudder down Maggie's spine.

He grasped her shoulders, and in the split second before he flipped her over, Maggie grabbed a high-heeled sandal from beneath the bed. Her attacker flung Maggie onto her back, sending her skull cracking against the floor.

Maggie persevered, slamming the shoe's heel into the man's face. He cried out in pain, and blood streaked down his cheek.

He backhanded her, making her teeth rattle and her

vision blur.

Maggie scrambled from beneath him, crawling across the floor, toward the French doors. Where was everyone? Had no one heard the man cry out? Had no one gone for help?

Loud music blared from outside and she remembered the sign from the lobby. A talent show had been scheduled for tonight around the pool.

Surely someone must have stayed behind.

She opened her mouth to scream, but her attacker was on top of her, sending her smashing into the door frame shoulder first. Pain exploded outward from the point of contact, and in the split second Maggie lay motionless, the man pinned her arms, working to free something from his pocket.

Maggie strained to see what he was doing, catching a flash of gold as he smiled. He waved a syringe before her face.

"A little something to make you more cooperative."

Adrenaline spiked to life in Maggie's veins. She bucked her hips in the same moment he flicked the tip of the needle with his fingertip. He lost his balance and Maggie rolled, taking him over onto his shoulder. Hard. The syringe skittered across the floor.

"You stupid—" he muttered as he lunged for Maggie again.

But she was already in motion, willing her body to remember every evasive move she'd ever learned.

Pounding sounded at the door. "Royal Cielo Police. Open up."

The man grabbed the syringe and was out the door, racing across the beach before Maggie could do or say anything. She forced herself to her feet, just as the door flew open. Eileen stood to the side, her face pale with fear. The first officer reached Maggie and pulled her away from the door.

"Outside." Maggie pointed. "Hurry."

"Do you require medical help?" the officer asked, a mix of excitement and worry tangling in his young eyes.

Maggie shook her head. "Just get him."

With that, the two officers were out the door and racing across the patio.

Eileen was at Maggie's side instantly, taking her face in her hands. "You need a doctor."

Maggie shook her head. "I'm fine."

"You're hurt. There's blood," Eileen said, her gaze riveted to the floor.

"His," Maggie answered, trembling so hard now she didn't think she'd ever feel warm again.

Eileen shifted her focus to Maggie's face. "Where did you hit him? Do you remember?"

"I sliced his cheek."

Eileen pressed her lips together, and her eyes softened, turning kind, reassuring. "Then they'll find him. Was it the man from the beach?"

"No." Maggie shook her head. This man had been larger, stronger than Sonny. "He wanted the ring."

"The ring the other man said he'd found."

Maggie shivered. "He did find it. I have it. It's Jordan's."

"We have to tell the police."

Maggie shook her head. "I think somehow they're in on it."

Eileen moved closer, pulling Maggie against her. She plucked a throw from the floor and dropped it over Maggie's shoulders. "You're in shock and you need to see a doctor."

Maggie couldn't remember the last time she'd been held by a friend, comforted, reassured. And then the tears came—the tears she'd sworn she was strong enough not to shed.

"What if I never see her again?" she asked, her voice barely more than a whisper.

Silence beat between them for a moment, but then Eileen answered, determination heavy in her tone. "You will."

"And if I don't?"

"Then you'll survive."

Maggie studied the woman, again filled with the sensation Eileen had suffered a great loss in her life.

"Who was it?" she asked.

Eileen laughed softly. "I guess my years in Cielo can't hide everything, can they?" She hesitated before she answered. "My brother."

"I'm sorry."

"He left for work one day and never got there. The police found his car parked next to a reservoir. They declared his disappearance a suicide so quickly my head spun."

"But you don't agree?"

Eileen sighed sadly. "My brother would never kill

himself, but the police were so fast to declare the case closed, I was never able to get to the truth."

"So you left?"

Eileen nodded, patting Maggie's hand. "I came here, and I know how you feel."

"They know more than they're saying," Maggie said.

"Are you sure?" Eileen's dark eyes softened.

Maggie nodded.

"How can I help? What do you need?"

Their gazes locked and Maggie felt their connection. Kindred spirits.

She knew in that instant exactly what she needed. She needed the one thing—the one person—who could make some sense of what had happened. She needed the one person who could help her find Jordan. Who could make everything right again, no matter what he'd done in the past.

She needed Will.

UPON THE team's arrival at Maggie's hotel, they separated. Kyle and Julian were to hit the beach, assessing the police activity and questioning witnesses. Lily and Rick would conduct guest interviews. Silvia had stayed behind at the safe house and at the ready should they need information.

Will headed for Maggie's room.

The door to the hallway had been smashed from its hinges, but the inside of the room had fared even worse.

The room had been fully ransacked, furniture

tossed, gutted, strewn across the room.

Will's focus dropped to a small trail of blood on the floor.

"Maggie!"

"She's in the bathroom." The female voice sounded from beside Will. He pivoted on one heel, spotting an attractive brunette near the closet, gathering Maggie's things.

She tipped her head toward the closed bathroom door. "They just got done questioning her. She wanted to take a shower."

"Is she hurt?" Will asked.

The woman shook her head. "Just scared."

"And you are?"

"My friend," Maggie answered as the bathroom door opened. Her long hair hung in damp waves. Her face had been scrubbed clean of all makeup, making her green eyes appear larger than usual in her pale face. "She's my friend."

Will read the fear in Maggie's eyes and the need for moral support.

"I'm very pleased to meet you," he said to the other woman. "Will Connor. I'm Jordan's father."

The woman blinked, apparently hearing about him for the first time. "Eileen Caldwell." She shook Will's hand. "I'm the resort manager."

"Have the police finished already?" He crossed to the door, spotting the telltale signs of fingerprint powder, but no other evidence the room had been processed.

"Random burglary. They believe Maggie came back

to the room at the wrong time. Another guest heard the struggle and called it in."

"But you don't agree?"

Maggie stared straight ahead as if her brain could no longer wrap itself around recent events.

"No," Eileen said, as she folded Maggie's clothing into a weekend bag. "I'm having another room made up for her."

But Will had an even better idea.

The attack on Maggie had been anything but random. Random would imply a coincidence and there was nothing coincidental about the events of the past two days.

Until the team knew who they were dealing with, Will wanted Maggie by his side at all times.

That meant only one thing. He had to move her to the safe house.

Ten minutes later, Eileen had helped him bundle Maggie and her belongings into one of the Body Hunters' cars. Maggie had agreed to the move more easily than he'd expected, and he knew why.

She was smart. Always had been.

Maggie knew as well as he did that her attack had nothing to do with burglary and everything to do with Jordan's disappearance.

Will had left the hotel manager with his direct line, making her promise to call if she saw or heard anything.

Maggie broke her silence as Will pulled out onto the street. "He had a gold tooth."

"Your attacker?"

She nodded. "And a syringe."

"Did he use it?" Will's every nerve ending jumped to attention.

"No." Maggie drew in a sharp breath. "He took it with him when he fled."

"Did you tell the police?"

She shook her head. "I don't trust them, Will."

"I can't say that I blame you."

"Do you think this is related to the explosion?" Her voice had gone flat, exhaustion edging into her tone.

"It might be," he answered honestly. "I'd like to call a doctor for you when we get back. Is that all right?"

Maggie nodded. "I'm fine, though. Just bruised."

She squirmed in the passenger seat and reached into her front pocket. "He knew about this." She pulled something from her pocket and handed it to Will.

His gaze dropped to the familiar band, the ring that had left an empty spot on his finger since the day he'd gone underground.

He pulled the car to the side of the road and cut the engine.

"It's Jordan's," Maggie continued. "She wore it around her neck on a leather cord. She's done so for years. But you wouldn't know that about her. You wouldn't know anything about her, would you?"

Shame washed through Will. Shame and regret. The heartache he'd fought to keep locked inside his soul for seventeen years threatened to explode. He shook his head without breaking his focus on the ring.

The puzzle pieces were beginning to float to the

surface. If he let himself be distracted by emotion now, he might miss a vital clue as to how the pieces fit together.

"How did you get it?" he asked flatly.

Maggie straightened in her seat, a renewed strength flashing in her eyes. "Sonny gave it to me."

Anger crashed through Will's system. "Why didn't you tell me earlier? Why didn't you give me this?"

The palpable tension between them simmered to a boil.

"Forgive me if I got a little distracted by your return from the dead and your covert band of operatives."

Will drew in a deep breath, focusing on regaining his cool. "Where did he get it?"

"He saw her struggle with two men the day she disappeared. He found this in the sand."

"Why didn't he give it to the police?"

"They didn't want it."

"I see." So Maggie's distrust of the Royal Cielo Police went deeper than her encounters with Commissioner Dunkley.

"Did he give you a description of the two men?"

She nodded. "One fits the age of Jordan's Jaime, but he didn't recognize him. The other is a man called Doc. He's involved in human trafficking, Will."

Will's heart hit his stomach.

Two mentions of human trafficking were two too many.

"We have a witness who saw two men put Jordan on a boat," he said.

Maggie whirled around in her seat. "Then we have to find that boat."

Will reached for her arm, surprised when she didn't pull away. "We found it. Jordan wasn't there, but we've narrowed down the possible region where she disembarked. And we know the owner."

Their gazes locked then, holding for several awkward seconds.

Maggie held out her palm. "I want that ring back."

Will didn't argue, pressing the band back into her palm. He was smart enough to know the gold band was no longer his to keep.

He pulled the car back out onto the road and pressed the accelerator.

"I want you to try to sleep. I'll brief the team on everything you've told me. We're going to find our daughter, Maggie. I promise."

"My daughter," Maggie said softly. "You haven't been her father for seventeen years, Will. Are you going to tell me you'll start now? Or do you plan to disappear back into hiding once this is all over?"

Will offered no answer, and Maggie's words reverberated in his brain as they drove toward the safe house.

How could he give Maggie an answer when he hadn't yet given himself one?

CHAPTER EIGHT

Body Clock: 45:25

Will slept fitfully in the bedroom's lone chair.

He'd insisted on having Maggie examined by a local doctor once they'd returned to the house. He trusted the physician, and the man had offered information on the person Sonny called Doc. Matter of fact, Doc was known to be Ferdinand King's medicine man, responsible for drugging King's victims.

Will shuddered at the thought of how close Maggie had come to being drugged and taken God knew where. But Jordan... Where was she? What had the medicine man done to their daughter?

After the doctor had determined Maggie's injuries were nothing more than bruises, Will had left her with instructions to sleep.

He'd checked in on her once, finding her sitting on

the patio, oblivious to his presence. He'd returned to the war room, where the team had worked the clues for hours.

When he'd come back a second time, Maggie had been sound asleep and he'd folded himself into the chair, content to watch her sleep.

Exhaustion had eventually won out over his efforts to remain vigilant.

Something brushed his forehead and then his cheek. Will blinked his eyes open to find Maggie kneeling in front of him, her fingertips tracing the lines of his face.

"Maggie?" He captured her hand in his, marveling at how natural the intimate move felt. "Are you all right?"

"I still don't understand how you could do it," she said softly. "I want to understand, Will. I just can't."

The sensation of her skin beneath his touch was almost his undoing. The years fell away and pressed against him at the same time. The deceit. The longing. The ceaseless inner turmoil.

He pulled her closer, sitting forward to wrap his arms around her. Her slender body felt firm beneath his fingers, warm beneath the cotton of her T-shirt. "I loved you. How could I not?"

Something flashed in Maggie's eyes—something far different than anger or hatred.

Desire.

Maggie's throat worked and she moved to pull away, but Will moved more quickly than she did.

He closed his mouth over hers, tasting deeply, his

body responding as her fingers found their way into the too-long hair at the nape of his neck.

Will pressed her lips apart with his own, his tongue tangling with hers, tasting the remembered sweetness he'd thought lost to him forever.

He trailed his fingertips down the length of her arms, interlacing his fingers with hers, helping her to her feet, walking her backward, until his body pressed hers flat against the wall. Her soft curves melded into the smooth planes of his chest and abdomen, and white-hot need coiled deep inside him.

A moan escaped from Maggie's throat and the heady sense of bringing her back to life threatened to overwhelm Will's senses.

He wrapped his hands around her waist then lowered his touch, cupping her backside and pressing her body fully against his arousal, his urgent want and need for her more intense than he'd imagined possible.

He raked his palms up her sides, caressing the bare skin beneath her thin nightshirt, pushing the fabric away until he found what he sought, cupping his palms over her breasts, thrilling to the sound of her sharp intake of air.

He dropped his kisses to her neck, then moved his mouth lower, across her collarbone then down to the valley between her breasts. He broke contact long enough to pull her shirt up and over her head, off her arms, then he sucked one nipple inside his mouth, teasing her flesh with his teeth.

Her knees buckled and he hoisted her into the air,

anchoring her legs around his waist as he pressed her bare back flat against the wall.

Her fingers worked his hair, her lips found the top of his head, his forehead, his ear, the line of his jaw, his chin.

Will nipped lightly at the soft flesh of her neck and Maggie's moan fed into the frenzy of his desire.

Will swallowed, taking a moment to drink in the sight of her. Maggie. His wife. The woman he thought he'd never hold in his arms again.

MAGGIE'S BREATH came in shallow pants. She couldn't remember the last time her heart had beat so entirely out of control, but the sensation of Will's hot mouth moving over her body was almost more than she could take.

Reality tapped at the base of her brain.

What on earth was she doing? Had she completely lost her mind?

Will closed his mouth over a nipple and teased her flesh.

Yes. She had lost her mind, and she had no plans to feel guilty about it. Not yet.

She raked her fingers through Will's hair, thrilled to the feel of his body pressing hers against the wall. His brute strength, his masculinity, his blatant desire —everything combined to put her on the brink of release before he'd even moved inside her.

Had she missed him that much? Had it been that long since she'd known a lover's touch? Yes.

Will carried her away from the wall, and sat her

on top of the bureau. He fondled her breasts, then lowered his mouth to the valley between them, trailing his lips down a slow, hot path to her belly.

She leaned back as he hooked his finger into her panties and slipped them down her legs. His mouth found her hot and waiting. His tongue teased her, and he slid his palms to her hips, pulling her against him.

Her head spun and she reeled with her impending release, not caring that she was about to lose complete control.

She'd found Will. Alive.

Alive.

He slipped one hand between them and stroked her as if not a day had passed since the last time they'd made love.

When Will reached up to tease her nipple all was lost, his fingertips at her breast, his touch inside her, his hot mouth exactly where she ached for him the most.

Maggie's orgasm crashed over her, and she gripped the sides of the bureau, holding on as her body pulsed with release.

Will broke contact long enough to carry her to the bed, lowering her gently onto the covers. He unzipped his jeans and stepped out of his clothing in one fluid motion.

He moved over her, easing his legs between hers, cradling her backside, pulling her to him as he slid inside.

The voice of doubt whispered again, but Maggie refused to deny herself the pleasure of making love to the man she'd missed every moment of every day for the past seventeen years.

They moved as one, rocking into each other, their breath mingling as they each gasped for air.

They were no longer two parents desperate to find their child, desperate to track down a madman before time ran out. In that moment, they were lovers, once lost, but now found. Together again as if they'd never been apart.

And after Will's body shuddered with his release and Maggie rode the wave of her second orgasm, she lay inside the cradle of Will's arms, protected from all rational thought.

Later, when the new day was nothing more than a lavender glow in the distance, she slipped free of his embrace, crawling out of bed.

She pulled her nightshirt on over her head and slipped into a pair of jeans, grabbing a sweatshirt from her bag.

She stepped onto the patio and settled into a chair, pulling her knees to her chest and hugging herself tight.

Had making love to Will been a mistake?

Could one night of lovemaking erase seventeen years of grief and pain and loss and betrayal? She knew it couldn't. She was no fool.

Yet, for one night, the years had faded away and she'd been transported back in time to what she and Will had once shared.

Love...and a life together.

But as the sky grew brighter and the day ahead grew

nearer, Maggie couldn't help but wonder.

Did the kind of love they'd once shared come around just once in a lifetime? Or could it be recaptured? Rekindled? Renewed?

She closed her eyes and breathed deeply, shifting her thoughts back to Jordan, where they belonged.

As for her and Will, only time would tell.

HE WALKED the beach, staring up at the starlit sky.

Cielo was such a beautiful setting for revenge.

He should probably make one final check on the girl, but the last dose he'd given her had been potent. With any luck at all, she'd sleep until tomorrow. Even if she didn't, where would she go?

He laughed, but his laughter gave way to a quick burst of annoyance.

Doc.

He'd given the man two assignments for the night. He'd achieved the first, making sure Sonny and his big mouth would be one less thing to worry about.

Doc had failed miserably at the second task, however.

He'd failed to deliver Maggie Connor and her daughter's ring. At least the police were under control. To his knowledge, they'd already declared the assault the result of a random burglary.

Perfect.

As for Maggie Connor, there would be other chances. He had no doubt.

But good old Doc had morphed from an asset to a liability.

He had no patience for incompetence. He hated it, actually. Hated it almost as much as he loved how close he was to making Connor pay for everything.

He'd intended to make Connor pay for his past mistakes with his daughter's life. But Maggie Connor's arrival on Isle de Cielo had sweetened the pot.

Revenge would be even more satisfying served family style.

And he couldn't wait to offer Will Connor his very first taste.

CHAPTER NINE

Body Clock: 51:15

Will and Maggie set out early the next morning and drove north toward Cielo's interior.

Based on information from the local physician who'd examined Maggie and on Silvia's crack research, they'd located the address where the man known as Doc had been born and raised. As best they could tell, his mother, Adele Jones, lived there still.

Today's target for the rest of the team was the southern quarter of the island and a door-to-door search for Jordan.

Will and Maggie drove in silence for much of the forty-five-minute ride. He couldn't help but remember how awkward things had been between them for days after the first time they'd made love. He'd never guessed history would repeat itself this many years later.

"Do you want to talk about it?" He cast a glance at Maggie, who had spent the drive intently studying the scenery outside the passenger-side window.

He'd awakened this morning to an empty bed, sending his heart racing, fearing the worst.

Instead, he'd found Maggie on the patio, staring at the gentle surf of the Caribbean Sea.

"Not now," she answered without turning to face him. "What do you expect when we reach the house?"

Nice change of subject, he thought. Fair enough.

"We need to get a local address for her son. A way to contact him. If he's the man who attacked you last night, whoever hired him isn't going to be happy. We need to find him and question him before someone makes sure he stays silent."

Maggie faced him then, frowning. "You think whoever he's working with would kill him?"

"Absolutely." Will nodded. "There aren't too many second chances in his line of work."

A tin-roofed house appeared around a bend in the road. Red door and shutters crisp and bright. Colorful laundry fluttered on the line and a shaggy mutt stood at attention at the end of a run, tail wagging.

The dog barked as Will pulled the car to the side of the road, but continued to wag his tail.

"He's either a good actor or a lousy watchdog." Will climbed out of the driver's door and rounded to Maggie's side. She'd already straightened out of the car and stood smoothing the front of her dress.

"Good boy," she said brightly. The dog's tail wagging sped to a frenzy. "Lousy watchdog." She smiled.

A jumble of scents filtered out of the home's front door. Eggs. Meat. Pastries.

"You're late," a woman's voice called out from inside.

Will and Maggie exchanged puzzled glances. The slight woman who appeared at the front step appeared surprised, then quickly shifted her features into a welcoming smile.

"Can I help you?"

"Adele Jones?" Will asked.

The woman nodded, pulling at the front of her patchwork apron. "And you are?"

"Maggie and Will Connor," he answered.

"Connor?" She twisted up her features.

"Our daughter went missing three days ago." Will closed the gap between where he'd parked the car and where Mrs. Jones stood. "We have reason to believe your son might have met her while she was on Cielo."

Mrs. Jones slid her hand to her throat. "*My* son?"

"An associate told us he was on the island for business," Will bluffed then glanced at Maggie. "Maybe we received bad information."

The older woman glanced back at the inside of her home, then to Will. "I haven't seen him."

"Were you expecting him for breakfast, Mrs. Jones?" Maggie asked. "We apologize for the interruption, but I'm sure you can understand how frantic we are to find our daughter."

Will watched as Mrs. Jones and Maggie locked gazes. The older woman's features softened instantly. One mother reading the emotional pain of another.

She pushed open the screen door. "Please, won't you come in? I'm afraid he's been delayed, but perhaps you'd like something to eat or drink?"

Maggie and Will climbed the concrete steps and followed the slight woman inside. The home was sparsely decorated but immaculate with bright splashes of color throughout.

"Your home is lovely," Maggie said, stepping toward a single framed photograph. "Your family?"

Mrs. Jones stepped to Maggie's side and pointed to the snapshot. "My brothers and sisters. There I am."

Will read the disappointment in Maggie's eyes even as she smiled warmly at the other woman. She'd hoped to find a picture of the son and had found siblings instead.

"Can I get you something?" Mrs. Jones asked.

"No." Will shook his head. His phone vibrated at his waist, but he ignored the signal. "Perhaps we could find your son another time. Does he have a favorite place to stay when he's on the island?"

A wistful look washed across the woman's face. "I'm afraid I don't know, Mr. Connor. I wish I could be more helpful. He's a busy man. A doctor." She smiled proudly. "He doesn't have a lot of time for his mother, I'm afraid."

"Do you have other children?" Maggie asked.

"No," Mrs. Jones said softly.

Will's phone vibrated again. Something had come up and he needed to check his voice mail, but he didn't want to do so here. He smiled at Maggie. "Perhaps we should be on our way."

Maggie jerked her thumb toward a short hallway. "May I use your restroom before our drive?"

Her comfortable manner with the older woman impressed Will. Maggie might have kept her contact with the outside world to a minimum over the past several years, but she was a natural when it came to making others feel at ease.

The other woman nodded, gesturing to a door just off the hall.

After Maggie excused herself, Will leaned closer. "I'm sure you can understand how difficult this has been for my wife." Will didn't have to force an emotional tone. His heartache was too real to hide at that point. "Are you sure you don't know where to find your son?"

The woman shook her head. "I'm sorry. No."

MAGGIE SLIPPED into the small bathroom and busied herself running the water in the sink then flushing the toilet. She cracked the door open, stealing a glance at where Will sat, deep in conversation with Mrs. Jones.

The woman nodded at whatever it was Will was saying, and Maggie knew instantly he'd won over her trust. He could do that. Make you trust him. Maggie should know.

Much as she hadn't wanted to open her heart to him again, it was already too late. Just watching him now, her body responded to him, wanted him, needed him. He was a part of her. He always would be, as much as she tried to claim otherwise.

She pulled the bathroom door shut behind her and

slipped down the hall to a bedroom.

Finely crocheted drapes hung at the open windows, and a hot breeze trickled into the room. The day was fast growing uncomfortably warm, but the beat of a ceiling fan kept the air moving in the small space.

Maggie headed immediately for the lone piece of furniture. A small bureau, adorned with a number of picture frames.

Will's voice grew louder from the sitting room, and she knew she had to move quickly.

She scanned the faces captured in the photograph, her gaze landing on that of one particular man.

So familiar, and yet, she couldn't be sure.

The man in the photo bore a horrible scar. She hadn't noticed a scar last night, but then, everything had happened in the blink of an eye and she'd been fighting for her life.

He appeared in most every picture, some alone, some with Mrs. Jones, one with a group of men. In none of them did he smile and she wondered if he were self-conscious about his gold tooth.

Will's voice rose in intensity and footfalls sounded behind Maggie. Her pulse kicked up a notch as she turned, finding herself face-to-face with the Adele Jones's puzzled expression.

"I'm sorry for the intrusion into your privacy," Maggie explained, her brain fumbling for an appropriate explanation for why she stood in the woman's most private space. "I spotted your photographs from the hall and thought they might be of your son." Moisture shimmered in her vision suddenly, honest and pure, not feigned. "I miss my daughter."

The older woman took Maggie's hands in hers, her touch cool but rough, hands that had seen a lifetime of hard work. "This is my son," she explained. "My Alberto."

Maggie watched as Will scanned the frames, his expression going from curious to tense in the blink of an eye. Had he recognized someone?

"My pride and joy." The older woman patted her heart.

Maggie's throat tightened. No matter what the man had done, he was this woman's son. Did she have any idea of the countless lives he'd damaged? And if so, did she love him anyway?

Mrs. Jones stopped in the hall at the sound of the faucet running in the bathroom.

Maggie pressed a hand to her cheek. "Forgive me. I'm not myself these days."

She waited until she and Will were in the car and on the road before she spoke. "Who was he?"

"Who?" Will couldn't fool her, not even after all these years apart.

"The man in the picture with her son. The one you recognized."

Silence beat between them.

"What makes you say that?" His tone tightened.

"I know you, Will," Maggie answered, shifting her focus away from the line of his jaw and out the window, where it was safer. "I always have."

Will exhaled slowly before he answered. "Montoya."

Montoya.

"The drug runner?" she asked. But wasn't he dead? Hadn't Silvia found proof? "I don't understand."

"He might be dead," Will answered, "but her son's got some tie to him."

"What do we do now?"

"We find Alberto Jones as fast as we can."

"What if he shows up after we leave?"

"I'll have Julian stake out the house." Will reached for his phone and winced. "I missed two calls while we were in there."

He accessed his voice mail and listened, his gaze narrowing as he listened. "It's Eileen. Dunkley's been looking for you."

"For me?" Maggie asked as he closed his phone and returned it to his waist.

"Sonny's dead," Will said flatly. "You're wanted for questioning."

DUNKLEY MEASURED Will and Maggie as they stepped into his office. "It appears you know each other, after all."

"We're recently reacquainted." Will held a chair for Maggie. "We understand you've found Sonny's body."

Dunkley studied Will then shifted his focus to Maggie. "Did you meet him last night after I asked you not to?"

Maggie opened her mouth to answer, but Will interrupted. "Other than the terrifying incident in her room last night, Mrs. Connor was with me. *All* night." Will's emphasis on the word "all" drew a smirk from Dunkley.

A pink flush fired in Maggie's cheeks, and Will knew he'd pay for the statement later. For now, he only cared about finding out how Sonny died, getting his hand on Jordan's file, and getting back to Silvia and her research skills.

There was no time for Maggie to endure questioning, least of all by Commissioner Dunkley.

"Fair enough." Dunkley snapped his mouth closed. "We do have a witness who spotted Sonny in Newmarket with a woman who matches your description."

Maggie straightened. "Surely I'm not the only blonde on Isle de Cielo?"

"Touché." Dunkley pointed to her cheek. "And that abrasion?"

"I was attacked, Commissioner. I'm sure you've read the report."

Dunkley sat back against his chair. "Most unfortunate, yes."

The commissioner paused dramatically before he turned his attention to Will. "I am not without connections, Mr. Connor, and I know you are far more than a private investigator. You head up a group called the Body Hunters? Am I correct?"

"I'm sure you'll understand if I don't answer that question." Will pushed out of his chair and shrugged. "If you don't need Mrs. Connor for anything else, we'll be on our way."

Maggie stood and turned for the door.

Will hesitated, deciding to work Dunkley for a few

moments longer.

"Mrs. Connor has decided to offer a substantial reward for any information that leads us to her daughter."

"How substantial?"

Will studied Dunkley's reaction, pleased at the way the commissioner's eyes brightened.

The man knew more than he was saying. Will had suspected so from day one, but the mention of money had drawn a most positive reaction.

"That depends on the information," Maggie answered smoothly.

"I'll keep that in mind." Dunkley patted his desktop then handed Will a folder. "Out of respect for your organization, I've prepared copies for you of the investigative notes from Jordan Connor's case. I'm sure you'll find everything in order."

"No doubt." Will turned to leave, placing his hand on the small of Maggie's back. He tapped his temple as if he'd almost forgotten to ask his next question.

"How did Sonny die, by the way?"

"Bullet hole between the eyes." Dunkley spoke the words without expression. "Most effective."

Will said nothing else as he and Maggie headed back outside. He drove out of the parking lot and down the road a stretch before he pulled to the shoulder, cutting the engine as he flipped open Jordan's case file.

He shook his head as he scanned the very thin contents. "*Is* everything in order?" Maggie asked.

"Sure is." Will cranked the ignition and slammed

the gearshift into First. "For a file that's been purged of any information we might have used. It's nice and tidy."

"What is it that man's hiding?" Maggie's voice echoed Will's frustration.

"I don't know, but we're sure as hell going to do our best to find out."

DUNKLEY SAT at his desk and ran one finger down the length of leather cord he'd removed from the Connor file.

With the proper tests, the strand of leather would no doubt yield a DNA connection to the neck from which it had once hung.

The neck of Jordan Connor.

He was being paid handsomely to destroy any physical evidence suggesting foul play in the girl's disappearance, yet the cord would do nicely as insurance.

If the powers that be did anything to threaten Dunkley or his position as commissioner, he wouldn't hesitate to bring the evidence forward.

After all, Mrs. Connor had just offered a reward for information, and this little item was likely the most concrete information the case had to offer.

He thought of the visit from Mrs. Connor after her first encounter with Sonny. Had the man done more than witness the Connor girl's abduction? Had he found something?

Dunkley shoved the thought out of his head. Sonny was a fool—a fool who had already been silenced.

He tucked the cord back into the evidence bag and slipped the package inside his desk drawer. If the opportunity to play both sides presented itself, he'd have a decision to make.

After all, insurance might not always be needed, but it was nice to be prepared.

Just in case.

CHAPTER TEN

Body Clock: 56:15

Maggie and Will had worked with Silvia long enough for Will to identify two of the men from Adele Jones's photographs.

Diego Montoya and Ferdinand King.

Additionally, running Doc's full name, Alberto Jones, had yielded interesting information. Not only was the man a key player in the King organization, but he'd been a soldier under Montoya.

Now the question remained, was Doc calling the shots? Or was King? And why?

Maggie had agreed with Will that Doc was most likely taking orders, and they'd placed King at the top of their suspect list, although they hadn't yet zeroed in on a motive.

Maggie held her breath as they approached the massive house, praying one more time that Jordan was still on the island and alive.

Over an hour's drive from the safe house, Ferdinand King's mansion was like nothing she'd ever seen.

As marble as Adele Jones's home was tin, as massive as hers was small, King's mansion was also as foreboding as her home had been welcoming.

Maggie had never seen such a blatant contrast of haves and have-nots.

Windows shimmered from every available surface, no doubt designed to take maximum advantage of the island's natural light and beauty. Yet the effect they gave to the outside world was no different than that of staring at slabs of ice, cold and unwelcoming.

Large stone pots brimming with multicolored flowers lined the drive, leading to a paved parking area and a set of wide, white stairs climbing toward white double doors, colored only by stained glass windows that perfectly matched the potted plants.

The rest of the home was as white as the staircase.

"Pure," she said in no more than a whisper.

"Hardly," Will answered. He pulled the car to a stop, slid the gearshift into Park, and cut the ignition. "Are you sure you're up for this?"

She nodded, even as her insides tossed and turned, her nerves pricking at the edge of her consciousness, holding her at a heightened state of awareness.

"I am," she said, releasing the clasp on her seat belt and pushing out of the car.

Two armed men stepped onto the landing at the top of the stairs, and Maggie's heart twisted, her insides going liquid.

Will, however, seemed completely unfazed, taking

her hand and leading her up the steps, even as the men stepped into their path, weapons visible.

"Good day, gentlemen," Will said, his tone genuine and authoritative. "My wife and I would like a word with your employer. Mr. King, I believe? Please tell him our interest concerns the disappearance of our daughter, and if Mr. King does not want a multitude of foreign media digging into his personal business, we'd ask for nothing more than ten minutes of his time."

One gentleman disappeared inside the house, while the second stepped to the middle of the landing, blocking any additional movement Will and Maggie might make.

They held their ground, Will balancing effortlessly on the second step, Maggie torn between retreating out of fear and crashing through the front door, demanding the man tell them exactly what part he'd played in Jordan's disappearance.

The first man reappeared. "Mr. King will see you in the solarium," he stated flatly. "Please follow me."

They followed the man through the massive home's foyer and hallway, each room they passed as colorless as the one before.

White marble floors led to white walls, white-trimmed windows, white curtains, white furniture.

It was as if the man had purposefully surrounded himself with white, thinking the clean color would purge the house, his life, and his soul of the evil he'd effected over the years, of the pain and heartache and broken lives he'd caused by dealing in human beings as if they were nothing more than disposable goods to be bought and sold.

The guard pointed to an open doorway and Will grasped Maggie's arm, tucking her protectively behind him.

She heard Ferdinand King before she saw him. "I'm sorry to hear about the girl. A runaway, from what I've been told," the man's voice boomed, strong and full of life, full of a confidence that belied no sense of surprise at their sudden intrusion into his home. "Please, come in."

He stood at an open doorway, an expansive veranda framing him, the Caribbean Sea sparkling behind him.

"Thank you for seeing us," Will said, crossing the room without hesitation to shake the man's hand.

King's eyes narrowed as he extended his hand toward Will. "But...we've already met, have we not?"

"Not likely," Will replied, sending Maggie's thoughts bouncing back to the past seventeen years Will had spent operating covertly from the Body Hunters compound.

"Ah, but I do know you." He shook Will's hand, his eyes never leaving his face. "It's been years, but you were once quite instrumental in bringing down one of my allies, were you not?"

Maggie's pulse quickened. Had King recognized Will from his former life? From the investigation that ran Diego Montoya out of business and into an early grave?

"Mack." King made a show of snapping his fingers. "Mack...something or other."

"Connor," Will said, filling in the gap. He extended his hand again even though the men had already gone through a formal greeting. "At your service."

One of King's white eyebrows lifted. "But I thought you said your name was Will?"

"A nickname," Will said flatly, his voice devoid of emotion. "And a name I've hidden behind for seventeen years, since your ally, Diego Montoya, threatened the lives of my family." He shook his head. "I'm not hiding anymore. So, you can tell whoever it is inside the Montoya family that has my daughter that if they want me, they can come and get me."

The surprise that had been simmering in Maggie's belly churned into a full-out boil of disbelief and anger. Was the man insane? Why not put a bull's-eye on his back and take out advertising on a billboard somewhere?

Was he *trying* to get himself killed?

And then she realized he was doing it again—doing exactly what he'd done all those years ago. He was deflecting the attention from Jordan to himself.

She'd seen the original note, the note he and Rick and the entire team had thought was from Diego Montoya until they'd discovered the man was dead.

But the fact remained that whoever sent the note wanted Will for some reason. Revenge, more than likely. And Will was apparently ready to offer himself up in order to save his daughter.

Again.

Her heart twisted in her chest.

Had she been completely wrong in refusing to forgive Will for deserting them all those years ago?

King's next words so stunned Maggie that all thoughts of her personal turmoil over forgiving Will flew out the window.

"You speak as if you believe the Montoya operation still exists, Mr. Connor."

Will arched a brow. "Are you telling me it doesn't?"

King moved to the open door that led to the patio, and the breeze ruffled the hem of his linen suit jacket. "Montoya's routes were absorbed by others the moment his dead body hit the floor. Doc came to work for me. The others—" he gestured toward the blue sea beyond where they stood "— scattered like sand on the beach."

"And why should I believe you?" Will asked.

King drew in a slow, steady breath then turned to face them. "The Montoya name is tinged only with disgrace now, my American friend. Suicide is not looked on lightly in my world."

"You speak as if you knew him quite well," Maggie said.

King nodded. "I took the name *King* not long after his death. The name of my birth no longer rang clean enough for a man in my position."

"The name of your birth?" Will asked.

"Montoya," King answered, a cool grin spreading across his face and turning Maggie's veins to ice. "My first cousin." He tapped a finger to his chin. "I suppose if anyone were out for revenge against you, Mr. Connor, for driving my cousin to suicide, it might be me, but I hold no ill will toward you." He tipped his head toward Maggie. "Or your family."

"What about Doc?" Maggie asked, planting her heels, suddenly determined she wasn't leaving this massive home without more information. "He used your boat to take our daughter. You just told us he works for you. How can you stand there and declare your innocence in my daughter's disappearance?"

Her boldness visibly took both King and Will by surprise.

King smiled, his amusement obvious. "Nicely done, Mrs. Connor. Nicely done."

He stepped toward her, but Maggie held her ground, steeling herself.

"Seeing as I've always been a man who places great importance on loyalty, I have no problem providing you with information on someone who's become a liability."

"You're admitting your man's involvement?" Will asked the question without emotion, and Maggie wondered how he could remain so calm.

He was all business, but then, he'd had nothing else in his life.

"Let's just say he's taken on projects outside my organization." A glint twinkled in King's dark eyes.

"Your human-trafficking organization." Will spoke the words as a statement, not a question.

The flash of anger in King's gaze was instant and furious. "I have no idea of what you speak, Mr. Connor."

"I'm sure you don't." Will thinned his lips. "But if this Doc person has overstepped his bounds, as you said, I'm sure you'll help us locate him."

King narrowed his focus, studying first Maggie and then Will. "You two look as though you enjoyed dancing together once upon a time."

Dancing?

Maggie bit back a laugh even as Will shook his head.

"I don't see what dancing has to do with—"

"There is a club on the eastern edge of the island." King cut off Will in midsentence. "The tourists don't know about it, but the locals can often be found there on a night such as this night promises to be." He gestured outside. "Cool. Calm. Perfect for a bit of adventure, wouldn't you say?"

"The name?" Will had already grasped Maggie's elbow and was steering her toward the door.

"Now if I told you that—" King laughed softly, the sound sending the small hairs at the base of Maggie's neck to attention "—you wouldn't have much of a challenge, would you?"

"Good day, Mr. King," Will said as they cleared the doorway, but then he stopped abruptly, turning so quickly he sent Maggie off balance. "There is one other matter, I suppose."

"Yes?" King had stepped onto the veranda, but now stepped back inside, his features invisible against the contrast of the bright sun behind him.

A faceless bully, Maggie thought. So perfectly appropriate.

"A man like Doc is a soldier, is he not?" Will asked.

"Utterly," King responded.

"If you're not calling the shots for him right now,

who is?" Will stepped back across the room, so close to King the other man bristled.

"You might try finding Montoya's son." King spoke the words slowly and dramatically, as if he knew exactly how shocking their implication would be.

"Son?" Maggie's voice grew tight. "But Montoya killed his son."

King stepped out of the shadow of the sun. "That, my friends—" He shook his head, pursing his lips "—is where you and your information are very wrong. My cousin's son survived the shooting, and I raised him as best I could. The finest schools Europe could offer."

Montoya's son was alive?

Maggie's pulse roared in her ears.

"How old would he be?" Will asked.

"Thirty," King answered. "Next month. Not that I expect to see him to celebrate. I haven't set eyes on the boy in over five years." He shrugged. "But what do you expect when you raise someone to be independent, let alone someone with Montoya blood."

Thirty.

Jordan had vanished after a week of dating a thirty-year-old. "Why are you telling us this?" Will asked.

King responded only with a wave of his hand, motioning to his bodyguard to show Will and Maggie the door.

"I have my reasons. Be very careful, Mr. Connor," he called out as they headed for the front door. "If the younger Montoya is the one looking for you, he is no doubt on Cielo right now, and no doubt watching every move you make."

JORDAN MOVED SLOWLY, testing her limbs, her fingers, her toes, as if somehow whatever injection Jaime had given her might have left a permanent imprint on her ability to move.

Her tongue stuck to the roof of her mouth, her lips were so dry she could taste blood where they'd split and cracked. She blinked, working to focus her eyes in the darkness. She glanced at the hole in the ceiling, spotting nothing but sky.

No sun. No moon. No stars. Nothing.

Despair welled up inside her, but she pushed herself off the wooden slab just the same. There was no telling when Jaime would be back, and no telling how long he'd been gone. If Jordan intended to find a way out, it was now or never.

She moved slowly, knowing there hadn't been anything but the wooden slab the last time she'd been awake, but she couldn't help but wonder if Jaime hadn't planted a trap for her, knowing exactly what she'd eventually do. Try to escape.

She slid her bare feet across the smooth stone floor, wondering when she'd lost her shoes.

Pack light. You won't need many of your clothes where we're going, Jaime had told her.

Bastard.

What an idiot she'd been.

Jordan took small steps, keeping her hands in front of her as she moved across the pitch-black space, unable to see anything. She shivered, chilled to the bone. Hunger had stopped pulling at her insides, replaced now by a hollow ache.

Why hadn't Jaime returned? Maybe this time he wasn't coming back. Maybe he'd only wanted to tell her lies about her father, to make her feel as low as she could possibly feel before he left her for dead.

Her hands hit up against one of the stone walls, and she began to work sideways, searching for a crevice, a crack, anything.

She worked to remember what the room had looked like the first day she'd awakened.

Stone. Stone floor. Stone walls. Stone ceiling. Considering the way Jaime had suddenly appeared, one of these must hide an exit. Maybe a secret tunnel. A trap door. Something.

What seemed like hours later, Jordan counted her fourth circuit of the room. She'd found nothing. Nothing at all.

And then she heard it. Footsteps. Echoes bouncing off walls nearby.

She fumbled, moving quickly to return to the slab, to hide the fact she'd been frantically searching for a way out. When the soft glow of a light illuminated the room, it did so not from the ceiling or a wall. It shone from the floor.

Jordan used the growing light to locate the slab of wood, launching herself toward it, sprawling flat on her back, closing her eyes.

She willed her breaths to come more slowly, more calmly, but even as Jaime entered the room, humming some tune beneath his breath, Jordan could do nothing to slow the excited beating of her heart.

The floor.

She'd never thought about an escape through the floor.

She listened, hearing the flick of Jaime's nail against the syringe and then the prick of needle to skin. As the darkness overtook her senses this time, she felt something she hadn't felt since the nightmare had begun.

She felt hope.

Because this time, she had a direction. She wouldn't be escaping up...or out. She'd be escaping *down*.

And next time, she'd make it out before Jaime came back.

CHAPTER ELEVEN

Body Clock: 63:50

T he night had gone cool, yet starless, calm, just as King had predicted.

The team traveled to the opposite side of the island in three separate vehicles, traveling together and yet very much apart.

Maggie self-consciously played with the sheer dress she wore, a loaner from Eileen's closet. Soft gauze ruffles edged the low-cut neckline, alternating rows of yellow and lime, blending seamlessly into the bodice of the dress, fitted and yet comfortable all at the same time.

Maggie had never worn anything like it, nor had she ever worn sandals quite so strappy, or quite so high.

Under other circumstances, she might feel like a princess, living a dream. Will was alive beside her and they were headed out for a night of dancing in a tropical paradise.

Reality tapped at the back of Maggie's brain. Ever present, ever vigilant.

Jordan.

Sixty-four hours had passed since her disappearance. Even Maggie knew that their chances of finding her daughter were running out.

If she'd harbored any false hopes about Jordan's chances, the solemn expressions plastered across each team member's face would have served as a harsh reality check.

Eileen had known instantly which club King had been talking about, saving the team research time. Much as she'd wanted to tag along in the hope she might recognize someone who had been at the hotel during Jordan's stay, Rick and Will had insisted on team members only, with the exception of Maggie.

"You look lovely." Will eased the car into a parking space.

Maggie noticed the other team members as they made their way into the club, but she did her best not to make eye contact, just as Will had instructed.

Silvia had accessed a satellite photo of the club and surrounding area, and the team had set their location assignments from the overhead shot.

Maggie and Will moved toward their assigned area now. The outside deck.

Strands of white lights dangled overhead, momentarily capturing Maggie's focus as Will steered her toward a table.

Julian brought them both drinks, earning nothing but a frown from Will.

"Appearances," the younger man said with a tight smile. "Aren't you always teaching me about appearances?"

A flash of something close to pride crossed Will's face. "So I am," he said. "So I am."

"Besides—" Julian grinned "—there's not a stitch of liquor in either of these."

As the young man walked away, vanishing seamlessly into the crowd, Maggie thought again about how natural the Body Hunters seemed, about how well they fit together.

They were the family Will had chosen. She and Jordan were the family Will had left behind.

She took a sip of her drink, cringing at the taste of the sickeningly sweet concoction.

Will lifted the drink from her hand, setting it on their table. "Let's dance."

Her pulse quickened as he took her hand in his. "I'm not sure that's such a good—"

"Best way to work the room without looking like we're working the room." He gave her hand a squeeze. "You might as well learn while you're here."

Whatever glimmer of attraction she'd felt at the touch of his hand faded at the know-it-all tone of his voice.

"How do you do it?" she asked, not caring that a couple next to them stopped midconversation at the sound of Maggie's raised voice.

Will responded only with a glare.

"Seriously." Maggie wiggled her hand free of his. "How do you shut off your emotions so effortlessly? I wish I could do it. I wish I could pretend our daughter wasn't God knows where at the hands of God knows who doing God knows what to her." Angry tears stung at the back of her eyelids and she blinked them away. "I wish I could pretend that finding you alive hasn't tipped my world on its axis, but I can't. How do you do it?"

A tear slipped over her lashes and she mentally berated herself. One thing she had no desire to show Will was weakness.

Instead of the lecture she'd expected, Will leaned into her, closing his arms around her waist and pulling her to him, pressing her against the hard planes of his chest and stomach.

His mouth closed over hers and his hands found their way into her hair.

His kiss was hard yet soft, lingering yet brief, and it left her head and heart spinning.

"Just dance with me," he whispered against her ear. "Don't think. Just dance like the first time we met."

They moved together across the dance floor, Maggie following Will's steps, not questioning his moves.

He slipped one arm around her waist and held her close, their bodies swaying to the island beat, their feet moving as if of their own volition.

"You dance as if you've done this a lot over the years." He spoke softly into her ear.

Maggie laughed, the sound nothing more than a quick exhale of tired breath. "It gets lonely night after night."

Will stiffened. "So you went out dancing?"

This time when she laughed, she truly laughed, the sound mixing with the voices and laughter of others at the club.

"No." She shook her head. "I played a lot of music. It felt good to move." She gave a quick shrug. "Good exercise."

A long silence fell between them, but the heat of Will's hand against her back burned through the gauze of her dress, putting her body on high alert, filling her with an urgent desire. She wanted to feel his hands on her bare flesh again, his lips on every inch of her body.

She swallowed, working to ignore the heat building inside her.

But then Will shifted her closer, sliding his palm up to her shoulder blade, pressing her breasts against his chest. Maggie settled into him, running her fingers up and over his shoulders, tracing the strong lines of his neck, finding the starting-to-curl-in-the-tropical-air hair at the nape of his neck.

Will inhaled sharply and she smiled, a heady sensation flooding through her. It may have been years since Will last held her this closely, since their bodies last moved as one on the dance floor, but she still knew her husband. Knew his body. Knew what he wanted.

Will wanted her. And she wanted him.

Will pressed his cheek against hers and brushed his lips against her ear. "All clear, quadrant three," he said softly.

Maggie realized that while Will's body might have

shifted its focus to her, his brain had never lost focus on their mission.

"Hold positions." He spoke again into the tiny earpiece each team member wore, only this time, his lips brushed her ear, then trailed down the side of her neck after he spoke.

Frustration burst the desire bubbling inside her.

She moved her palms to his chest, pushing away from him, turning away, not wanting him to read the disappointment in her gaze.

Someone moved in her peripheral vision. A man. A shadow. A shadow so like the shadow from her hotel room she held her breath.

"Where?" Will asked, twirling her behind him, out of harm's way.

Maggie looked around his shoulder, catching the profile of a lanky man, deep in conversation. The voice filtered to her across the space as if the volume had been turned down on every other voice in the room.

Her attacker's voice.

The man laughed in response to something another man in his group had said and gold glinted in his smile.

"There," Maggie said, tipping her chin.

TENSION RIPPLED through Maggie's body.

Will spun her away from whatever it was she'd seen, putting himself between her and any potential threat.

"Where?" he asked again.

"Group of three. Khaki jacket."

Will scanned the crowd, zeroing in on the group and the man in question. He was a perfect match to the photographs of Alberto Jones.

Doc.

Adrenaline sliced through Will's veins. "Q3 possible sighting."

Finding Doc was the team's first concrete step toward finding Jordan, and Will would do whatever necessary to make sure they didn't blow the takedown.

Will maneuvered Maggie farther away, not wanting the man to spot her before the rest of the team was in place, but as Rick, Julian, Kyle and Lily flawlessly slipped into the surrounding crowd, Doc lifted his gaze, like prey sensing the predator.

His cold stare locked with Will's and he smiled, the party lights strung overhead glinting off a single gold tooth.

Will fought the urge to charge the man, to tackle him to the ground, to strangle him with his bare hands. Instead he waited, moving Maggie even farther away, waiting until Rick and Julian had moved past Doc, the team now bracketing the man on all sides.

"Stay here," he whispered, making a show of tucking Maggie safely into a chair and handing her a drink.

As he turned to walk away, she wrapped her fingers around his wrist, the intensity of her grip taking him by surprise.

"We have to get him, Will." Their eyes locked, and in the depths of Maggie's pale gaze, Will spotted her desperation and her love for their daughter.

"We will."

He broke away from her touch, ignoring the sense of loss at not having her in his arms, not having her by his side. He strode across the dance floor, nodding quickly at Kyle as his footsteps ate up the distance between him and where Doc stood.

This time when their gazes met, something other than amusement flashed in the other man's eyes. This time, recognition dawned.

A split second later, Doc was on the run, racing through the crowd, crashing into one table and overturning a chair as he slipped beyond the wall of the club and onto the beach, darkened by the moonless night.

"Move, damn it," Will snarled into his piece. The team's responses sounded instantly.

"I'm on him."

"Headed south."

"We've got to cut him off before he reaches the trees."

The trees.

Will raced across the club floor and onto the beach, his shoes sinking into the powdery soft sand. A hundred yards down the beach a stand of palms loomed, palms that would provide more than ample cover for Doc on a night like this one, without a moon or stars to give away his position.

The team raced across the beach, gaining on Doc's shadowy figure, but not before the man slipped into the grove of palms.

The moon slipped out through a break in the clouds, sending light across the beach in eerie synchrony to the waves, crashing against the shore after their journey over the Atlantic.

Will's heart pounded in his ears. This was their break. He could feel it.

A successful apprehension of the man called Doc would lead them to Jordan. It had to.

He raised his weapon, tipping his chin toward Julian and Lily as he nodded in one direction, then toward Kyle and Rick. The team scattered, moving methodically through the trees, closing in on their prey.

A cove lay just beyond, and if Silvia's research on the area was correct, a series of caves began here on the east side of the island, running for miles underground through a series of passageways and ravines.

A man born and raised on Cielo—like Doc—would no doubt know every inch of the caves. He had to be stopped before he reached the entrance.

Moonlight flooded the area, casting shadows from the massive palms. Will pressed himself against a tree, scanning his surroundings, looking for any sign of movement.

A footfall scuffed the sand behind him, and he whirled around, gun trained at eye level.

Maggie's stunned face met him head-on.

He lowered his weapon, grasping her arm and shoving her against the tree as he covered her with his body. Even now, at a time like this, he was aware of her heat, her pulse, the softness of her skin beneath his touch.

"What the hell are you doing here?" he whispered in her ear, working to control his fury. He couldn't afford to let his temper be the reason he blew his position.

"She's my daughter, too."

"Stay here." He spoke the words directly into her ear, pressing his lips to her hair. "Do not move. Not for any reason. Understood?"

He pulled back, and Maggie glared at him, not giving an answer.

He scowled and she nodded. He pressed her to her knees, gesturing for her to pull herself as small as she could, and then he was off, moving methodically through the palms. One tree at a time. Operating on nothing but instinct to move him closer and closer still toward the answers Doc offered.

A woman screamed. Then another.

Clouds covered the moon once more and Will froze momentarily, working to get his bearings. Another scream cried out. He was in motion, racing toward the sound before his brain kicked in. The scream hadn't been that of a woman.

Cielo was famous for monkeys. Wild, screaming monkeys.

He blew out a sigh of relief just as the moon peeked out again, this time for several long seconds. Long enough for Will to see a man ahead.

The figure moved again, and Will's gut tightened at the realization that the man moved toward him, gun drawn, glinting in the light of the fickle moon.

The moon vanished, casting the entire area into a pitch-black so thick Will swore he could reach out and touch the darkness.

"Will, he's on you," the communicator in his ear chirped. "Drop."

Will had no sooner dropped to his knees than the sickening *thwap* of a bullet sank into the tree above his head.

But who had issued the warning? Rick?

"I've got a visual. I can take him."

Julian.

Will prayed the months of training had been enough. He couldn't bear the thought of losing the young agent to a dangerous operation such as this one.

"Hold," Will murmured. "We need him alive."

The moon shifted once again from behind the clouds, washing Will and his location in white light.

Another shot sounded and then a second.

Too close together to have been from the same gun.

"Subject down."

Julian's voice.

"Are you hit?" Will called out as he hit the ground running.

"Negative. But he doesn't look good."

Voices sounded from all directions. His team. Running. Shadows in the night. Emerging from the trees, converging on the spot where Julian knelt, fingertips to Doc's wrist.

Will knew at first glance that all hope of taking Doc alive had been lost.

Julian lifted his worried gaze to Will's face. "I had to take him. He had you in his sights."

Will merely nodded. Julian had made the only choice possible. He'd saved Will, and for that, Will would be forever grateful.

Doc murmured an unintelligible stream of words, the incoherent murmurings of a dying man.

Will dropped to his knees, needing to press the man for information while he could still speak. "Where is she?" he asked, gripping Doc's bloody shirt.

As the other man's pallor faded and the life slipped from his body, he spoke again. "Closer... closer."

Julian shook his head, pulling his fingertips away from Doc's wrist and dropping the man's arm to his side.

"He's gone." Julian shook his head.

Will checked the other's man pulse, finding none. When he patted Julian's shoulder and looked him in the eyes, what he saw there stopped him cold.

He saw nothing. No trace of emotion. Nothing but vacant, brown eyes.

Shock.

"You had no choice." He gave Julian's shoulder a squeeze. "Taking a life is never easy, but you had no choice."

Julian nodded, but his gaze remained empty, devoid of any sign that Will's words had gotten through.

Will pushed to his feet, stepping to Lily's side. "Shock," he said under his breath.

"I'll take care of him."

"Where's Maggie?" Rick asked, his breathing as

steady as if he'd never left his seat back at the club.

As if on cue, Maggie stepped to Will's side, pressing her hand to his chest, searching his face. He shook his head, and she sagged before his eyes.

Closer.

Doc's words teased at the base of Will's brain.

The cruel irony was they weren't any closer to finding Jordan. If anything, now that Doc was dead, they'd lost their one real shot at information.

Will felt further away from finding Jordan than he had in the past three days.

He reached for Maggie, pulling her into his arms. He worked his fingers into her hair, tipping her head against his shoulder, pressing a quick kiss to her forehead.

"We'll find her."

But even as Will spoke the words, time was running out.

If this screwup hadn't just cost them all the time they had left.

ECHOES OF VOICES filtered in and out of Jordan's dreamless state.

Voices. She tried to wake herself. Voices.

Maybe someone was near the hole, near enough to hear her.

Try as she might, she couldn't force her eyes open, couldn't force herself to speak.

Help me, she screamed inside her head. *Help me.*

Yet she could make no sound. She could utter no plea for help.

"He's gone," someone said. A voice so eerily familiar she wanted to cry, yet no tears came.

And so she fought, fought against the altered state of consciousness that had wrapped itself around her brain and refused to let go.

"Where's Maggie?"

Maggie.

Her Maggie? Mom?

Had she come to Cielo? Did she know Jordan was in trouble?

"We'll find her."

Another voice. A shadow from her past. So far away and yet, so close.

Jordan tried to think, tried to make sense of what she was hearing, but her drugged and dehydrated brain refused to cooperate. The blackness clawed at her, pulling her back from the brink of lucidity.

Help me, she screamed again in her mind. *Help me.*

The voices fell silent, and she began to sob, emitting nothing more than a choked cry only she could hear.

Her time was running out.

If she didn't find a way out of her prison soon, she never would.

CHAPTER TWELVE

Body Clock: 68:20

Kyle had driven Maggie back to the safe house, where she now waited for the rest of the team to return. She'd pumped Kyle for information, but the quiet man had offered nothing other than a gentle reassurance the team would locate Jordan.

Maggie sat back against the headboard in Will's room, tired of pacing out of frustration, amazed once again at the secret life her husband had led after his supposed death, as well as before. During the early days of their marriage, he and Rick had set the Body Hunters' organization into motion.

Two men with nothing but business training and determination had recruited, trained and mobilized a team of private citizens who had apparently made one hell of a difference to a lot of families who'd written off their loved ones as lost forever.

Amazing.

Maggie pushed off of the bed, pacing once more, then stopping, zeroing in on Will's personal belongings, or should she say, lack of personal belongings.

If the top of the bureau boasted everything the man had brought to the island, he owed his rugged good looks to nothing more than a comb and a stick of deodorant.

She smiled, tracing a finger along the edge of the comb, remembering the first time she'd run her fingers through his hair, remembering how amazing it had felt to fall in love with the man, to exchange marriage vows, to deliver their child.

Her stomach tightened, the memory of dancing in Will's arms earlier tonight sending a shiver of awareness through her.

Making love to him the first night they'd been back together might have been a mistake, but there was no denying Will's touch had brought a part of her she'd thought dead forever back to life.

She tugged at the dresser drawers, filled with the sudden urge to know everything about Will. What clothes he wore. What he dreamed about. Who he'd loved.

The first drawer revealed nothing but boxers and socks, the second nothing but T-shirts, separated by color. So Will. Controlled and compartmentalized.

Were those the attributes he'd tapped into when he'd decided to "die"?

Maggie pressed on, sliding open the third drawer, her fingers stilling at the sight of what lay inside. A photo album, worn around the edges.

She hoisted the object from the drawer and headed back to the bed, settling against the pillows before she cracked open the front cover.

Her breath caught at the sight of herself. A photo taken at the trial of the man accused of planting the bomb that had killed Will. He'd never been charged with Will's death, but he'd been found guilty of four other murders. When he'd been taken out of the courtroom, headed for a life without parole, Maggie had felt justice had been served, even though it had been an empty justice without Will.

Now she wondered just how real the threat from Montoya must have been to have driven Will to set up another man, guilty of other crimes or not.

She flipped through the pages, her gaze drinking in the photos, clippings, articles—all documenting her life with Jordan.

She touched her finger to Jordan's face—as a young girl, a preteen, a high-school senior. Maggie's heart squeezed, sitting heavy inside her.

For the past two days, she'd thought Will heartless at his ability to leave her and Jordan behind, when it now appeared he'd never left them behind at all.

During all of the years she thought him dead, he'd followed their lives, knowing them from a distance, always present but out of sight.

He'd cared.

Could she find it in her heart to forgive him for what he'd done?

Voices sounded in the hallway and Maggie scrambled, jumping from the bed to return the album to the drawer. She knew Will well enough to know he hadn't shared a prized possession such as the album with the rest of the team.

Will would view such sentimentality as a sign of weakness.

Maggie viewed it as anything but.

Her thoughts overwhelmed her, flooding her with emotions. The loss of Jordan. The reunion with Will. Working alongside the team. The remembered image of Doc's dead body on the beach.

Her head spun and she rushed for the bathroom, slipping inside and shutting the door behind her. She slid to her knees, unprepared for the strength of the sobs that racked her body, cranking the sink's faucet to hide the sound of her crying.

She'd spent half her life hiding from the outside world, fighting to shelter her daughter from risk of any kind.

In just a few days, she'd lost her daughter and experienced a harsh reintroduction to the big, bad cruel world outside. The reality was almost more than she could bear.

Tonight another woman had lost her child. A grown man capable of evil, yes, but someone's child just the same. Mrs. Jones's child would never come home alive.

Would Maggie's?

The last was the unknown that broke Maggie, sending her down to the cold tile, curled into a ball, arms wrapped around herself. Afraid of what lay ahead.

Even more afraid of what might lie behind.

"Maggie?"

The bathroom door cracked open, and Will stepped inside, worry painted across his handsome features.

Maggie was on her feet and in motion before she could give so much as a second thought to what she was about to do.

She wrapped her arms around Will's waist, buried her face against his neck, savoring the feel of him, the scent of him, the heat of him.

And in that moment she knew one thing. She wanted Will more than she'd ever wanted anything or anyone in her life. She wanted to lose herself, wanted to forget that Jordan was out there somewhere, scared, alone, maybe hurt...or worse.

She wanted Will to take away the pain, the heart-ache, the worry.

She wanted...Will.

Nothing more.

WILL BUNDLED Maggie into his arms, holding tight. He pictured the moment back on the beach when he'd spun on her, gun drawn.

Instead of protecting her from his world, he'd given her an up-close-and-personal glimpse of how danger-ous—and deadly—life could be.

Who was it that wanted to hurt his family after all this time? Montoya's son?

Will couldn't think of another who would want him so badly. Sure, he'd been responsible for putting away numerous criminals during his time with the Body Hunters, and any of them might want him dead, but none knew about Maggie and Jordan. He'd been adamant about keeping his history secret.

Only Montoya, their first target, had known about Will's past. So whoever was behind Jordan's kidnapping was somehow tied to Montoya.

He had to be.

The son made perfect sense. But where was he? And who was he?

Maggie shifted in Will's arms and his body responded. Even now, exhausted, frustrated and at a loss for how to proceed next with the investigation, Maggie's presence pulled at him, teasing him out of the protective wall he'd so carefully nurtured for so long.

Will stroked her hair, closing his eyes, inhaling her scent. "I'm sorry you had to see that tonight."

"I just keep thinking of his mother," she said softly. "That poor, poor woman. She loved him so."

Will grimaced. He hadn't stopped to think about the mother. He should have known Doc's death would send Maggie's thoughts to the other woman.

"I'd like to go see her," she said, as if reading his thoughts.

Will shook his head and cupped her chin with his fingers, forcing her focus to him. "No."

Her green eyes narrowed. "What do you mean, no?"

"No," he repeated. "From this point forward, you do not leave this house. Understood?"

"Will, I'm perfectly—"

"No." This time, he gripped her shoulders and gave her a gentle shake. "I can't protect you out there, and I can't afford the distraction."

Maggie's brows lifted, as if his words had taken her by surprise.

"You shouldn't have been there tonight."

"But what if you'd found Jordan and I wasn't there?" She searched his face.

"We didn't."

"What if you had?"

Will hated the heartache he heard in her voice, wanted nothing more than to ease her pain. "I'd have brought you to her as quickly as I could."

"She needs me, Will."

He nodded. No point arguing with that logic. "She needs you alive."

He pulled Maggie close, so close he could feel her breath on his face. "I need you alive."

"You never really left us, did you?"

Maggie pushed back from his embrace, studying him intently.

Will frowned. "I'm not following you."

"The album." Her eyes widened.

The album. She'd found Rick's album.

Will had never been a good liar. Not as a kid in grade school. Not now as a grown man facing Maggie, presented with the opportunity to regain her trust by simply telling a small lie about the photograph album.

"It's not mine," he said flatly. The truth. Always the truth.

Maggie took a backward step. "What do you mean?"

"It's Rick's."

"Rick's?"

Will reached for her, but Maggie rejected his touch and stepped around him, back into the bedroom.

"He thought I'd want it one day." Will followed her, keeping his distance.

She spun on him, her expression wounded. "But you didn't want it?"

Will shook his head.

"What the hell is wrong with you, Will?"

What *was* wrong with him? Why hadn't he sought Maggie out years ago? Why hadn't he called the house? Stolen a glimpse of their lives?

Because he'd been afraid he'd never be able to leave once he saw them again. "I was dead. I had to stay dead. But I'm here now, Maggie."

"Are you?" She hurried toward the door, jerking it open.

"Maggie—"

"Don't worry," she called out over her shoulder. "I'll stay in the house."

He thought of following her, but didn't, understanding her need to get away. And as he watched her hurry down the hallway, he could only think one thing. Whoever had said "the truth shall set you free" had been a complete and total idiot.

MAGGIE LET herself into the bunker, let the silence wash over her.

The overhead lights had been left on and several coffee cups sat partially full on the long table as if the team had just left, no doubt to grab what little sleep they could before they regrouped in the morning.

She walked toward the various boards mounted on the wall. Slowly. Tortuously. Forcing herself to step ever nearer to the chart of suspects, the lines drawn between photos, the scribbled notes, the slash through Doc's name.

Jordan smiled brightly from her graduation picture, her long blond hair gleaming beneath her emerald cap, tassel proudly tossed to the side.

"Oh, baby. Where are you?"

Maggie sank to her knees, exhaustion and fear taking hold and sucking the remaining strength from her body. She sat in that position for a long time, praying for so many miracles her mind spun.

She prayed for Will or Rick or Kyle to burst through the door to tell her Jordan had been found alive. She prayed for Will to say he was sorry, to tell her he'd put the album together, to tell her he'd been wrong to leave them.

Yet here she sat. Alone. Surrounded only by the specter of Jordan's disappearance and the shadows of theories and hypotheses on where Jordan might be, if she were even still alive.

"What is her favorite color?"

The female voice took Maggie by surprise, and she lost her balance, shifting abruptly to one side.

A slight hand reached out to her, and she looked up into Silvia's kind eyes. "I didn't mean to frighten you," the other woman said.

Maggie took her offered hand then climbed to her feet, sitting in the chair Silvia pulled out for her. "I overreacted," she gave a dismissive wave. "I'm sorry. It's been a long day."

"Honey—" Silvia dropped onto the chair next to her and patted her knee "—it's been a long week." Her gray brows furrowed. "Can I get you anything?"

A knot of emotion clogged Maggie's throat. "My daughter."

Silvia shifted her hand to Maggie's shoulder, squeezing tightly. "Don't you doubt it for a minute. I've never seen this team more committed to bringing someone home."

"Thanks." Maggie patted Silvia's hand but shifted away, breaking the contact. "Why are you still awake?"

"Waiting on a report to run." She tipped her chin toward one of the computers. "Thought I'd come down to see how it was going. I'm glad I found you, though. I'm ready to piece together Jordan's quilt and I want to make sure she'll like the colors. Will didn't know the answer when I asked him."

Quilt?

"Answer?" Maggie asked, her head swimming.

"Jordan's favorite color." Silvia's eyes widened expectantly. "I quilt to relax, and I'm working on a design for Jordan."

"That's very kind." Maggie thought again about the question and smiled, remembering all of the times Jordan had refused to name just one color when asked the same question. "She likes them all."

"All of them?"

Maggie nodded. "She loves rainbows."

Silvia's features brightened with her smile. "Then it's rainbows she'll get."

As Maggie looked into Silvia's eyes, she added to her prayer list, praying the other woman was right.

CHAPTER THIRTEEN

Body Clock: 74:30

When Will woke the next morning, Maggie was nowhere to be found. He looked for her on the patio, along the beach, but found no sign of her.

He headed for the kitchen, but found no one but Rick, sitting alone, sipping his coffee. Trepidation tapped at the base of Will's skull. "Have you seen Maggie?"

Rick pursed his lips. "She probably took off after that fight you two had."

Will winced. "You heard us?"

Rick sighed. "Buddy, the whole island heard you."

Will poured a cup of coffee then paced the small space.

"Where would she go?" Rick asked.

"Maybe back to the hotel. She seems to have gotten friendly with the manager." Then he thought of something Maggie had said right before their argument.

He snapped his fingers.

"She wanted to see Alberto Jones's mother."

"Doc's mother?"

Will nodded, heading toward the hall.

"Will," Rick called to his back. "What the hell *is* wrong with you?"

Will turned around, Rick's question taking him by surprise. "What?"

"How could you live knowing they were alive somewhere without you?"

Tired of the accusing glances and the doubts, Will bolted for his bedroom. He slipped the frame from between the mattress and box spring and reversed his steps.

He set the framed photograph in the middle of Rick's breakfast. "It was easier to live knowing they were alive, than knowing they were dead."

Rick stared at the photo of Maggie and Jordan. "I was out of line."

Silvia barged into the kitchen, her face pale. "It took all night, but I found Montoya's son." She handed Will a printout. "Every search I did on Diego Montoya, Jr., came back with his death certificate, but when I searched aliases associated with Ferdinand King, I caught a break. The photo is seven years old, but there's no doubting the identity."

Will stared down into the familiar face. The brown

hair. The goatee. The emotionless eyes.

How had he not seen the resemblance to Montoya before?

He rocked back on his heels, squeezing his eyes shut, and Rick snatched the picture from his hands.

Rick's expression shifted from disbelief to anger to steely determination. "Where is he now?"

"His room's empty." Silvia shook her head, her voice cracking. "He's gone."

MAGGIE PULLED the car to a stop just outside the rusty gate, noticing immediately that something was different about Mrs. Jones's home. The shutters had been pulled closed. No wash hung from the line out back and her dog's chain was gone.

Had the woman picked up and left?

But why? Because of their visit? Because of her son's death?

She'd lived her entire life in this house. Surely she wouldn't let her son's scandal run her off the island.

"Mrs. Jones," she called out tentatively. No response.

Maggie stepped cautiously toward the porch steps, her heart catching at the sight of the front door slightly ajar.

Fear began to tap at the base of her brain, but she shoved it away. The older woman had merely neglected to catch the latch on her way out, that was all.

Yet as Maggie climbed the concrete steps, anticipation choked her. Was there a more sinister reason for the older woman's absence? Had she come to harm?

Maggie swallowed, taking a steadying breath before she pushed against the door, waiting as it opened with a squeak.

"Mrs. Jones," she called again. Still nothing.

Inside, the house appeared as it had been. Spotless. Tidy. Sparsely furnished and brightly decorated.

The older woman had probably gone to visit family, Maggie tried to reassure herself, moving slowly through the living space. An irrational need to check the house filled her, wrapping itself around her and moving her forward.

She needed to know Adele Jones hadn't been harmed, needed to know what had happened. She had her answer when she crossed the threshold into the bedroom.

The bed had been made and the closet door stood open. No items of clothing hung inside. The framed family pictures that had lined the top of the handmade dresser were gone.

Not a single personal item remained behind.

Mrs. Jones was gone. And Maggie could only hope she'd gone of her own free will.

She turned to leave, crying aloud at the sight that met her.

Julian stood in the bedroom door, smiling.

Will had been worried. She should have known.

"Will sent you?" she asked. "I'm sorry you had to come all this way for nothing. She's not even here."

But Julian said nothing. He merely smiled.

Maggie moved to step around him, and he moved sideways, blocking her path.

"What are you doing?"

"I came back to lock up."

Maggie's brain worked overtime. Julian had killed Mrs. Jones's son. He no doubt had felt the need to apologize. He'd probably arrived just in time to help her with her things.

"You helped her move?" she asked, wanting so badly to hear him say yes, but suddenly fearing he was about to say anything but.

She swallowed down the irrational thought. He was a team member. A Body Hunter.

He nodded, and Maggie breathed a sigh of relief.

"We'd better get back."

She tried to step around him again, but this time, he wrapped his fingers around her upper arm so tightly she cried out.

"You're hurting me."

"That's funny." Julian laughed, the sound sending the small hairs at the base of Maggie's neck to attention. "That's exactly what your daughter said."

The magnitude of Julian's words barely registered before he shoved her to the floor, pinning her wrists behind her back and beneath his knee as he pulled something from his pocket.

A syringe.

Maggie struggled to free herself, to throw Julian off balance, but he was too strong, too big.

"You'll never get away with this. Will will come after me. He'll figure out what you've done."

What had he done? To Jordan? To Mrs. Jones? How had he gotten inside Will's organization?

Who was he?

Questions and emotions tumbled through Maggie's mind, fighting for position. Then one emerged, alone. Urgent. More important than all the rest.

"Jordan?" she asked.

"Is she alive?" he asked in return. "Did I hurt her? Rape her? Sell her into slavery?"

His words sliced through Maggie's heart like a butcher's blade, and tears stung her vision. "You'll never get away with this." She forced the words through the knot of anger and fear clogging her throat. "He'll find us."

"Who?" Julian asked, flicking the needle with his fingernail. "Will?"

Instead of waiting for Maggie's answer, he stabbed the needle into her upper arm. She cried out, and he laughed, long and loud, like a man who knew he was in complete control.

"You know, he left you once. You'd think you and your daughter would get the point. Or do you need me to spell it out for you?"

Confusion swirled through Maggie's brain. "What are you talking about?"

She reached for the bedspread, seeking leverage, but achieving nothing more than pulling the cover to the floor.

"He walked away from you once. What's to keep him from walking away again?"

Maggie slid toward unconsciousness. As hard as she tried to move, to struggle, her limbs failed to respond to her brain's wishes.

She could only hope Julian was wrong about her husband. She could only hope the glimpses of love she'd seen in Will's actions and expressions were just that. Love.

And maybe this time, he'd make a different choice when it came to saving his family.

Maybe this time Will would stay and fight until the bitter end.

CHAPTER FOURTEEN

Body Clock: 76:10

The moment Will set eyes on the Jones house, he knew he and Rick were too late. The house sat shuttered and the property appeared fully deserted, yet the front door sat open wide.

"He's already got her," Kyle said, slamming a fist against the dashboard.

Much as Will valued the man's intuition, he wasn't about to admit Maggie had become a victim without proof.

He had that seconds later.

The bedspread had been pulled from the bed and Maggie's purse lay kicked beneath the bed.

Will swore under his breath just as his cell rang. He glanced at the caller ID display and shot Kyle a quick look. "It's him."

"We could trace the signal." Kyle reached out a hand, motioning for Will to wait.

Will shook his head, flipping the phone open. "We'll play this your way. Where is she?"

Julian's laugh filtered across the line, exploding a hot ball of anger deep inside Will's gut.

"The more important question for you is, where am I?" Julian asked. "Without me, you've got nothing."

"You have them both?" Will kept his voice flat, his emotions in check. The effort took every ounce of control left in his body.

"I'll tell you when I see you."

"Where?" Will asked, raking a hand through his hair.

Another laugh, this one doing nothing to hide Julian's contempt. "If I were you, I'd think about praying. Somewhere sacred. Say three o'clock?" He hesitated before his next statement. "Oh, and Will? Leave the rest of the gang at home."

The line disconnected.

Will's mind whirled with possibilities.

Somewhere sacred?

Julian's words bounced through Will's brain. A church? A monastery? There had to be countless such places on the island. But where?

He turned to Kyle. "We've got less than six hours before the meet to figure out what he's talking about."

Kyle gave a tight nod and headed for the car.

Will held out a hand, tipping his chin toward the

keys in Kyle's hand. "I'll drive."

THIS TIME, when Jordan regained consciousness, she forced herself off of the slab of wood. She stumbled when her feet hit the cold floor and she gripped the bed to steady herself.

Lowering herself to her knees, she ran one hand over the floor. Stone. Dry stone.

Where was she?

She fumbled across the floor, dreading what she might crawl over, or touch, but the floor was surprisingly dry and clean, as if Jaime had swept it in preparation for her stay.

Jordan laughed. Her *stay*. Now that was funny.

She worked her way toward the side of the room where she'd seen Jaime enter. Working methodically, she splayed her fingers, not wanting to miss the slightest hint of an opening.

When the fingers of her left hand hit up against a crack, her entire body tensed. Jordan pulled herself to her knees, running her hands over the area, a thrill shooting through her at the realization she'd hit some sort of board instead of rock.

Her eyes slowly adjusted to the gloom, aided by the narrow stream of daylight pouring through the chamber's ceiling. She worked as quickly as she could, pulling at the edge of the board, lifting the piece of pressed wood and sliding it away, over the floor, to reveal an opening. Small, but not impossible to climb through.

She moved carefully, painfully aware of her weakened state, lowering herself feet first. She hit a second floor more quickly than she'd anticipated, without having to hang or drop from the opening.

Jordan moved away from the opening, losing the weak glow of sunlight from her prison, but finding something else.

Fresh air. Warm on her face.

She'd read about caves back at home and thought they were cool, dank places, covered in slime, but so far, this cave—if that was, in fact, what this place was —appeared to be anything but.

She carefully stepped along the passage, running her hands along the smooth wall, taking small steps, hoping against hope she wouldn't misstep and end up injured...or worse.

Something sounded in the distance, a sound Jordan hadn't heard before during the time she'd been imprisoned here. She closed her eyes and concentrated, willing her brain to wrap itself around the sound, to identify it.

A tinkling noise. A dripping noise. Like a musical instrument...or something.

And then Jordan realized the noise was coming from something even more beautiful than a musical instrument. The noise was coming from water.

There had to be an underground stream or creek nearby. And if she could only find it and follow it, she might find a way out. A way to find the voices she'd heard the last time she was awake.

A way to freedom.

The dripping noise persisted, sounding more like a

small stream now than a leak. Jordan pressed forward, her pulse quickening.

The wall curved away from her hand, and the floor dipped. As Jordan rounded the bend in the passage, she saw it.

A pool of water at the base of a small waterfall.

She blinked, stunned at finding such a beautiful site after days of the ugliest experience of her life.

She hurried forward, never having been so thirsty in her life. She dropped to her knees, savoring the feel of the lip of the pool against her bare flesh.

Jordan leaned forward and her hair fell into her face. She shoved the dry, lifeless strands away, caring only about one thing.

Her first drink from the stream.

But then she heard it. A scraping noise. Footsteps. The drone of unintelligible muttering.

Jaime.

Jordan reached longingly toward the water, but pulled her hand back, realizing she couldn't afford to get wet. If Jaime discovered she'd found a way out, he'd kill her. It was that simple.

She swallowed down her disappointment and turned, hurrying back the way she'd come, praying she'd reach the small room and her bed before Jaime spotted her.

She hoisted herself up through the small space and slid the board back into place, just as Jaime had left it, amazed at how bright the small chamber now seemed in comparison to the passage outside.

Sunshine streamed in through the hole in the ceiling and she smiled. Soon, very soon, she'd turn her face up to that same sun as a free person. She knew it. She believed it.

Jaime struggled with something at the doorway and Jordan moved, scampering onto the wooden slab, willing her heart to slow, shutting her eyes and doing her best to appear unconscious.

Yet, when Jaime entered, it wasn't Jordan on which he focused. He muttered continuously, dragging something across the floor.

Jordan remained perfectly still, fighting the urge to steal a glimpse at whatever it was he'd brought with him. Countless images from too many horror movies flashed through Jordan's mind, but when Jaime repositioned her, then placed something next to her, the reality of just what he'd brought into the chamber was far worse than any scene from a movie.

Jordan recognized the scent of her body lotion. The feel of her slight shoulder and arm. The strand of long hair so like her own, that fell across Jordan's face.

"Sleep tight," Jaime said. "Looks like your precious girl's slipped into an unconsciousness all her own. I'm sure you two will have a lot to catch up on when you wake up. *If* you wake up."

Jordan waited, holding her breath, until she heard the slide of the board. She forced herself to count slowly to fifty, lying still until long after Jaime's footsteps faded away.

Then she opened her eyes and slowly turned her head, reaching out to touch the woman she'd taken for granted for too long.

"Mom," she said softly, choking on a mix of joy and fear.

She'd been afraid she'd never see her mother's beautiful face again, but now that she could see her and touch her, an entirely different fear filled Jordan's heart.

If her mother was here, trapped beside her deep inside this cave, who was on the outside looking for them?

WITH SILVIA taking the lead, the team worked feverishly back at the safe house, researching religious chapels, churches and gathering places.

After tracing the varied histories, Silvia projected satellite images of the island onto the one bare wall, and the team narrowed their choices to three.

When the doorbell rang, surprise registered in each face.

"I'll get it," Kyle said.

Will followed him up the steps, hanging back as the other man opened the door, allowing Eileen Caldwell access to their inner sanctum.

"What is she doing here?"

Kyle answered without apology. "I called her."

Will spotted something in the other man's eyes he'd never seen there before. A glimmer of attraction.

"I can help." Eileen stepped toward Will. "If Julian used the word *sacred*, I know exactly where you'll find him."

Will pinned Kyle with a glare. "You shared that with her?"

The other man said nothing.

This time when Eileen moved, she moved between Will and Kyle, her gaze locking with Will's. "Maggie is my friend. Let me help."

"She knows the island better than we ever will." Kyle spoke softly, intensely.

Will thought for a moment, realizing Kyle and Eileen were right. Kyle had followed his intuition in bringing the hotel manager here.

"Downstairs."

No other words were spoken until the three had joined the others.

Eileen studied the satellite maps and the three locations the team had chosen. She shook her head and pointed at a spot on the map they hadn't considered. "The Abbey."

Will stepped close. "That's nothing but a cliff."

"Exactly." She smiled. "A naturally occurring chapel. The locals consider it the most sacred ground on Cielo."

Sacred.

"How long to get there?" Will asked.

"About an hour from here."

"I'll drive." Kyle took a step away from the screen.

"You're going to need help." Eileen pulled herself taller. "It's not easy going. The Abbey's at the top of a cliff in a densely vegetated spot."

Will stared at her long and hard. The woman was not a team member, but she had the obvious spirit of a fighter, and she'd become a friend to Maggie.

"Let's go then," he said, not looking back to see the

faces of the team behind him. Let them think he'd broken the cardinal rule about no nonteam members on an operation simply because the body was his daughter.

Truth was, he'd broken the rule because Eileen could put him on location faster than anyone else.

And time was something of which he had precious little.

MAGGIE AWAKENED slowly to the sensation of someone stroking her cheek. "Will?"

But then she recognized the featherlight touch, recognized the frightened breathing pattern.

"Mom?"

Jordan. Thank God. Her baby was alive.

Maggie forced her eyes open, shock slicing through her at her daughter's battered appearance.

Jordan was alive, but heaven only knew what she'd been through.

"Oh, honey." She pulled Jordan into her arms. "I was so afraid I'd never see you again."

"Where are we, Mom? Who's going to find us?"

Maggie stroked her hand over Jordan's hair, tightened her hug. "I don't know where we are, but your father will find us. Don't you worry."

Jordan choked out a gasp, pushing free of Maggie's grip. "So, it's true?"

Maggie hated herself for not softening the blow about Will's survival. "Who told you?"

"Jaime."

Jaime. Otherwise known as Julian. "Did he hurt you,

honey?"

Jordan shook her head. "How could Daddy do that to us?" She choked on the words.

Maggie took her daughter's hands and sighed. "I'll explain it all to you, but we have to forgive him for what he did. He saved our lives."

Jordan's features crumpled.

"Come on." Maggie scrambled to her feet, pulling Jordan along with her. "I have no doubt he's on his way to save us now, but let's get you out of here, just the same. If we can find a way out of this room, we're bound to find a way to the outside."

Jordan's next words landed like a soothing balm on Maggie's soul. "I already know how."

EILEEN STUMBLED on a vine and Will swore under his breath. He hadn't looked at the woman's wedge heels when he'd agreed to let her lead him to the Abbey. If she didn't break her neck before they reached their destination, it would be a miracle.

"How many times have you been here?" he asked, climbing expertly, noticing the protective hand Kyle kept outstretched toward Eileen's back.

"I've been here once." Eileen's ankle rolled and she went down in a heap. "Damn it." Embarrassment fired in her cheeks. "We're almost there. I'm sure of it."

Will stood his ground as Kyle helped the woman to her feet. The Atlantic surf crashed nearby.

Eileen Caldwell was right. They were close. And Julian had told him to come alone.

He stepped around the pair as Kyle checked Eileen's

battered ankle. "I'll take it alone from here."

Kyle glared at him, and Will read the unspoken disapproval.

"Hold ground," Will explained. "I can't afford to anger him, you know that."

Eileen said nothing, looking from Kyle to Will and back again.

"Fair enough." Kyle pulled his gun from the back of his waistband and dropped to a ready position. "Just give the signal and I'm there."

Eileen's dark eyes had gone wide.

Will gave a sharp nod and set off toward the sound of the surf, toward the man who had betrayed his trust. The man who had kidnapped his daughter and his wife.

A few moments later, the dense vegetation thinned, and the outcroppings of rocks became more numerous. Will had no sooner spotted what appeared to be a stone chapel, when Julian spoke.

"We meet again."

Montoya's favorite greeting.

The young man stepped from behind the altar, gun trained on Will's face.

Will's pulse roared in his ears, a tangle of anger and frustration raging inside his chest. "Diego Montoya, Jr., I presume."

Julian grinned, though no emotion showed in his dead eyes. "I prefer Jaime, actually. So much for your ability to read people, no?"

He was the picture of his father in that moment. Heartless. Ruthless. Without a soul. How had the similarities slipped Will's notice?

"Where are my wife and daughter?"

Julian made a tsking sound with his mouth. "Not so fast, Mr. Connor. I call the shots today."

He waved his pistol toward the cliff. "Let's move this little party, shall we?"

He stepped away, and Will followed, thinking of how easy it would be to put a bullet into the back of Julian's skull.

But he'd do no such thing, and Montoya's son knew it.

Truth was, Will was at the young man's mercy if he ever wanted to see his family alive again.

Julian stepped to the edge of the cliff, studying the cove below before he turned to face Will, his evil grin spreading wide.

"So, Will. Tell me, are you ready to find out how it feels to lose everyone you love?"

CHAPTER FIFTEEN

Body Clock: 82:00

W ill thought of going for his gun, of trying to wound Julian, but he knew he couldn't risk the outcome. Much as it pained him, he had to play the young madman's game.

He could see the flash of insanity in Julian's eyes.

Like father, like son.

"I lost everyone I loved once," Will stated matter-of-factly. "I don't plan to lose them again."

Julian shrugged. "Perhaps this time, the choice isn't yours to make.

"I wonder if you can imagine what it's like to stare down the barrel of your father's gun just before he shoots you." Julian unbuttoned his shirt, revealing the angry scar. "Here's where he missed."

"He wasn't in his right mind." Will took a step closer as Julian focused on his old wound.

Julian waved his gun at Will, then trained it on the

space between Will's eyes. "I have you to thank for that. Oh, and I don't plan to miss, if you're wondering."

"He was evil, Julian."

Julian smiled. "Don't worry, he wasn't exactly your biggest fan, either."

Will slid one foot closer to the spot where Julian stood.

The young man laughed. "You seem to forget who trained me, Will. I'm ready for your moves."

"Tell me where they are, Julian." Will held up a hand as he spoke, as if his palm could slow any bullet Julian might fire. "Help me and I'll help you. Things are always easier if you cooperate. Commissioner Dunkley will help."

"Commissioner Dunkley is dead."

Julian's words stopped Will cold.

Julian grinned, the expression so evil ice ran through Will's veins. "Seems he had a little evidence on the side he thought he could use to his own advantage." He shrugged. "I let him know he was wrong about that."

"I know you, Julian. This isn't you."

One corner of Julian's mouth lifted. "You don't know me at all." He tapped the gun to his forehead then aimed at Will again. "You know who else you don't know? Your daughter."

He whistled. "She's quite beautiful. It's a shame she'll never know the pleasures a man can give. I should have accommodated her before she died. She wanted me to. Did you know that?"

Fury boiled in Will's gut, but he battled to maintain control, to rise above Julian's verbal taunts.

Julian bit down on his lip. "Although, she wasn't very happy with me after I told her the truth about you. I understood, though. I know how it feels to find out your father doesn't want you around."

Will lost complete control of his senses, not caring that Julian held a gun on him. He charged, hitting the other man below the belt, sending them both crashing onto the unforgiving ground.

He heard the breath escape Julian's lungs and knew he had to hit him again. Hard and fast. He grabbed the hand holding the gun, smashing Julian's forearm against a rock.

The gun hit the ground with a thud, sinking into the sandy underbrush.

"You destroyed my family," Julian hissed, his voice taking on a tone of evil Will had never heard there before.

"Your father destroyed your family." Will ducked to avoid a punch and misjudged, taking a glancing blow to the side of his face. He spun on one heel, raising his arms defensively as Julian came at him head-on.

Their bodies connected, pain exploding outward from the point where Julian's fist connected with Will's kidney. They went down together onto the sand and rocks, rolling, tumbling, maneuvering for position.

The glint of the late-afternoon sun against the barrel of Julian's gun caught Will's eye but he reached too late.

Julian gripped the gun, rolling into motion, landing on his feet and pushing himself upright.

Will scrambled to his feet, reaching for his weapon, but found it gone, apparently dislodged by the struggle.

"Lose something?" Julian laughed.

Will circled, arms outstretched, ready to defend himself against any attack Julian might dish out except one—the bullet that would come from the barrel of Julian's gun.

"How did it feel to fake your death and disappear?" Julian asked.

"Hardest decision I ever made," Will answered.

Julian snapped his tongue. "You know, it wasn't that difficult to find you." His brow furrowed. "The so-called serial bomber contacted my father's cousin. Seemed he never really believed you were dead. He thought my family might be interested in that fact.

"Once I tracked down your former business partner and your family, all I had to do was wait and watch. I'd heard rumblings about the existence of the phantom group of do-gooders, the Body Hunters. I was amazed at how easily you welcomed me into the fold." He gave another shrug. "You really should be more careful.

"Then I waited for your beautiful wife to let the lovely Jordan out of her sights just long enough to grab her. Imagine my delight when she traveled to Cielo. A week in paradise."

Julian's grin turned Will's veins to ice, then he

pursed his lips. "When your wife followed, my revenge became even sweeter than I'd planned. Imagine."

Will scowled, not liking the fact he had no control over the situation. He had to outmaneuver Julian and get his gun. There was no other option.

"Suppose I killed Jordan and Maggie?" Julian asked, taking a backward step, adjusting his aim. "I wonder how you'd cope."

"I'd find you and kill you."

Julian's features fell flat. "What if I was already dead? You'd have no course for revenge."

Emotions tumbled through Will, battling for position even as his brain tried to make sense of Julian's words.

"If you were dead, Maggie and Jordan would be rescued."

"Not if you never found them."

Julian grinned again, and this time the expression sent a shudder of dread racing down Will's spine.

"Taking a life is never easy, even when it's necessary." Julian spoke the words as he eased his aim. "Isn't that what you said?"

The glint of evil Will saw in Julian's eyes was so pure he knew nothing he could say would touch the young man's heart or soul. There was no reasoning with someone already dead inside.

"You'll never find them." Julian shook his head. "They'll die in their hole like two caged animals."

"The Body Hunters will find them. They won't stop just because you kill me."

Julian spat, the move a vulgar rebuke of the Body Hunters and their ability. "Trust me, I wouldn't waste a bullet on you, Will."

Julian placed the barrel of the gun to his temple. Adrenaline pumped to life in Will's veins. "What are you—"

"Revenge, Will. I'm going to take away the thing you love even more than your family. Control."

Will launched himself into motion as Julian's shot exploded.

Motion stilled. Time slowed.

The life left Julian's face the instant the bullet hit home. His body toppled over the edge of the cliff, falling like a stone toward the cove below. He landed with a sickening thud on an outcropping of partially submerged rocks.

As Will watched the first wave crash over Julian's lifeless body, he said a prayer for the soul of the young man he'd mentored, trusted, cared for.

Then Will reached for his communicator, needing to send the team into action even as he stayed to deal with the authorities here.

Diego Montoya's son had made a vital mistake.

They'll die in their hole.

He'd provided Will with a single clue.

And a single clue was all the Body Hunters needed.

CHAPTER SIXTEEN

Body Clock: 83:15

Maggie struggled to gain her bearings. She held on to Jordan for dear life, not wanting ever to let go again.

Jordan pointed toward the corner of the room. "There's a board and a hole. I found a passageway."

Maggie scrambled across the room. She hooked her fingers beneath the edge of the board and slid it free, revealing a small hole, just big enough for an adult to fit through.

Jordan had moved to her side.

"Do you want me to go first?"

Jordan shook her head. "I will. I've done this before."

A few moments later, they both stood in the passage below, breathing heavily.

"Which way?" Maggie asked.

Jordan pointed. "There's a waterfall. I think it leads

outside."

Outside.

Exactly what Maggie wanted to hear.

But Jordan frowned as they neared the flowing water.

"What's wrong?"

"It's bigger than before." Jordan scowled. "I'm sure of it."

"What's bigger?"

"The waterfall. The pool."

"Maybe the tide's coming in." Maggie dipped her fingers into the pool then tasted the water. "It's salt water. We must be on the east side of the island."

She lifted her gaze to Jordan's. "A series of caves starts on this side of the island and runs halfway across." She held out her hand, waiting until Jordan took it. "That must be where we are."

Jordan slipped her hand inside Maggie's. "So we follow the water?"

Maggie nodded. "We'll follow the water."

They moved slowly in the dark and narrow space. The floor sloped upward, along the side of the falling water. But if Maggie wasn't imagining things, the flow of water had increased, splashing droplets as it cascaded downward back to where they'd started their climb.

The passage narrowed and sight became even more difficult.

Maggie felt for a ledge, somewhere to climb, something that might lead them up and out of the cave. She pushed up on her tiptoes, running her palm along the stone until she found what she wanted—a ridge, jutting out from the wall.

Excitement flickered through her and she moved more quickly, reaching up onto the stone shelf as far as she could. Her fingertips brushed against an object. A long, smooth object.

She held her breath. Touching tentatively, she slid her fingertips down the length of what felt like bone.

She withdrew her hand and jumped, hoping to get a glimpse of what lay hidden above their heads.

She saw nothing, but jumped again.

This time, she caught a glimpse of the object, and her blood ran cold.

"I need something to stand on."

"Use me." Jordan dropped on all fours, making her back level.

Maggie shook her head. "You're battered and bruised enough."

"Do it, Mom. We've got to find a way out."

Maggie didn't have the heart to tell her it wasn't a way out she wanted to get a better look at.

She stepped onto her daughter's back, pressing her palms against the wall to shift as much weight as she could off Jordan. "Are you all right?"

"Fine." Regardless of what she said, the strain and exhaustion in Jordan's voice were unmistakable.

Maggie blinked her eyes, letting them adjust to the darkness of the recessed space.

A human skeleton lay on its stomach, one arm extended over its head, as if the victim had died trying to crawl out, trying to escape the same prison in which Maggie and Jordan were now trapped.

A scream ripped from her throat and she fell, tumbling backward toward the unforgiving stone and water below.

"WHERE'S KING?" Will charged past the guards at the mansion's front door.

The authorities had finished questioning Will about Julian's death and, based on the suitcases lining the curb next to a limousine, word had reached King.

"He's already—"

"I'll see him." King cut short his bodyguard's reply.

He stood just inside the foyer, his typically pristine linen suit crumpled. Apparently beating a hasty departure didn't lend itself to maintaining a calm, collected appearance.

The arrogant glint in his eyes was missing, and Will allowed himself a moment of sympathy.

"I'm sorry for your loss."

King shrugged, gesturing toward the veranda. "The boy was lost to me years ago. I've got ice water on the patio, if you'd care to join me."

Will followed behind the man. "Looks as though you're planning on staying away for a while."

"Forever, actually." King pushed open the patio door, letting Will pass. "There's nothing here for me on Cielo. Not now."

What about your slave trade? Will wanted to ask, but didn't. For the time being, he needed King's cooperation in pinning down possible island locales where Julian might have stashed Jordan and Maggie, but he'd already made a silent vow to himself.

A man who made his millions trading in human lives didn't deserve to go unpunished. But that was a pursuit for another day. Another time.

"The police believe he took your daughter?" King asked.

"And my wife," Will replied. "Commissioner Dunkley is missing. It's amazing how quickly the rest of the force has changed their tune about the investigation."

King shrugged. "The island way."

"Which is actually why I'm here to see you." Will stepped to the railing, drinking in the view, so breathtaking it appeared surreal. How could so much beauty exist in a place that harbored such evil?

"You want to learn the island way?" King asked.

Will shook his head, turning to lock stares with the older man. "I want to learn the island. As Montoya's son knew it. Where would he put them?"

"As I understand it, the police have begun a door-to-door search."

Will nodded. "But you and I both know he wouldn't have done this the easy way. He told me he put them in a hole."

"A hole?" King took a backward step.

"A hole," Will repeated. "Where is it? You'd never make a great poker player, I'm afraid, Mr. King."

King picked up a pitcher of ice water and poured two glasses. Will fought the urge to swipe his arm across the table, smashing the glass and ice against the tile floor. He maintained control, knowing the lives of the two women he loved more than anything depended on him playing the man before him for information.

King held out a glass and Will took it, wrapping his fingers around the heavy glass.

"I brought the boy here after he healed from his father's shooting." He drew in a slow breath, held the glass to his lips, but then lowered it to the table without drinking. "He was—" he hesitated "—never the same again."

"After the shooting?" Will asked.

King nodded. "He had been a kind child once. A boy with a heart." He pressed his lips into a tight line, then grimaced. "He never showed any evidence of a heart again."

"And the hole?"

"Years ago, the government of Cielo decided they could tame the maze of caves beneath this island for profit. They blocked some of the tidal flow, closing off certain areas and opening others."

Will had seen the advertisements during the few days he'd been here. Tours. Tram rides. Underground waterfalls. Additionally, he knew one series of caves started not far from where Julian had shot Doc.

King smiled, the move slight and bitter. "His preferred cave was not far from the Abbey."

"I need more than that." Will set his glass on the table, moving toward the door. The instant King gave him a location, he planned to be in motion.

"I'm afraid I can't give you an exact location for the entrance, but I can tell you that he used to stay away for days at a time. There were a series of disappearances years ago. Family pets. A young girl."

The tension coiled inside Will snapped, unfurling at breakneck speed.

"A young girl?"

"A local." King breathed in slowly. It took every ounce of restraint Will possessed not to go for the man's throat. "The consensus was that she committed suicide or drowned."

"But?"

"But I could see it in his eyes. He'd had a part in it."

"And then you sent him away, didn't you? Did you ever tell the police?"

King shook his head. "It wouldn't have helped that girl."

"It might have helped her family."

Will's mind raced back to the Abbey and the surrounding area. He'd need a satellite view, but the cove where Julian had killed Doc couldn't be that far away.

"Do you know if the cave had access to the ocean?"

King's brows furrowed. "I know the tidal flow had been diverted somehow, but our housekeeper used to complain of wet clothing periodically."

Will didn't wait to hear anything more. The information wasn't much, but it was something. "Until next time, Mr. King."

"Next time?" King asked.

But Will didn't offer a response.

He was out the door, in his car and on the phone in a matter of seconds, mobilizing the team. He needed Silvia to pinpoint cave entrances along that stretch of beach and structural alterations that had been made by the government.

In the meantime, the team would split up and begin the search.

With any luck at all, they'd locate Jordan and Maggie before they ran out of daylight.

Before they ran out of time.

PAIN RIPPED through Maggie's hip and thigh as she connected with the cave floor. "Mom!" Jordan scrambled to her side. "What happened?"

"We have to go back."

"What?"

"Now." Maggie forced herself to her feet, grabbing Jordan's hand and pulling her back the way they'd come, fighting the image of the skeleton burned into her brain. "We have to move. Now!"

"What did you see?"

"Nothing."

"Nothing?"

Jordan twisted around, rising up on her toes trying to spot whatever her mother had seen. The darkness and height of the ledge saved her from the gruesome sight.

Water lapped at the sides of Maggie's feet and she realized they had even more serious problems than finding a skeleton.

Panic unfurled inside her, threatening to take over every ounce of focus she had left. She forced herself to think, forced herself to breathe. "Jordan, did the room where Jaime kept you ever get wet?"

Jordan shook her head.

"Then we have to go back. It's the only sure way to keep you safe. When the water recedes, we'll try again. We'll go the other way."

"No," Jordan cried. "He'll find us."

Based on the speed at which the water was rising, Maggie knew they'd likely drown before Julian came back, if he ever came back at all.

She pulled Jordan along beside her, running a hand along the wall to steady herself.

By the time they'd descended to the level of the pool, the water had reached the walls and they waded shin-deep.

She pictured the chamber and the glimpse of the hole she'd seen in the ceiling.

A hole in the ceiling.

As they reached the entrance to the chamber, she reached for Jordan, prepared to help hoist her through the opening.

"I cannot believe we're going back," Jordan muttered.

Maggie gripped her shoulders and stared into her daughter's eyes. "This room will either be high enough to keep us dry or the water will push us up to the hole."

"Are you crazy?" Jordan twisted up her features.

Probably, Maggie thought, but she'd rather be crazy than dead.

And as she waited for Jordan to clear the opening so that she could climb back into the prison Julian had prepared for them, she focused on Will. Focused on the team.

If ever there were a group of people that could reach her and Jordan in time, it would be them.

The water pushed at her thighs as she scrambled through the hole, and she sent Will a silent message.

If he ever wanted to see his family alive again, he had to do only one thing.

Hurry.

CHAPTER
SEVENTEEN

Body Clock: 84:20

A ccording to the information Silvia was able to glean from Cielo archives, a system of underground passages not far from the site of Doc's shooting had been the area first targeted as a tourist attraction years earlier.

While sea gates had been installed to control the flow of each high tide at the single sea-facing opening, and an emergency access door had been placed somewhere on the ground above the caverns, no additional development had taken place.

Apparently the surrounding terrain in a second location had been easier to tame.

There were two choices for approach. Follow the beach and search the cove at the sight of Doc's shooting. Or approach the rocky terrain above the cove by passing through a nearby sugar cane plantation.

The team chose both.

Silvia's words reverberated in Will's mind as the team split up.

I've put a lot of sleepless hours into Jordan's quilt. Go bring that daughter of yours home.

Home.

A word he'd never thought he'd use again in connection to Maggie and Jordan. But if they all survived —when they all survived—he'd ask Maggie for a second chance.

He'd stop trying to keep his emotions in check.

He'd live. He'd feel. He'd love.

If she'd have him.

Will and Rick, both with experience in caving, headed for the cove, while Kyle and Lily followed the higher ground, searching for any sign of the rumored emergency access.

The cove was a far different place in the light of day than it had been the night of Doc's shooting. Only a narrow strip of sand lay between the ocean and the stand of palm trees.

"High tide," Rick said.

"Could have lived without that." Will scanned the surrounding coral outcroppings, searching for any sign of an opening.

Neither he nor Rick voiced the obvious concern. What if the location where Julian had stashed Jordan and Maggie wasn't above sea level?

Will shoved the thought away, refusing to let the

deadly image play with his mind.

He had to focus. Had to think. Had to move.

And then he saw it. A shadow beneath an outcropping of rock, so dark it had to be an opening.

"There." He pointed. But Rick was already on the move, scaling the uneven coral, moving with an unshakable determination.

He stopped when he reached the entrance, letting Will lead the way.

As Will shimmied through the small space, water surged through a much larger opening below.

He could only hope that wherever Maggie and Jordan were, they were high and dry.

MAGGIE STOOD on the board Julian had used to cover the chamber's entryway, hoping against hope she could stem the flow of rising water. Her efforts appeared to be futile.

The water had reached the middle of her shins and the board had begun to sag. At this rate, it wouldn't be long before she and Jordan would have to start treading water.

"Are you sure the water never came in like this before?" she asked Jordan.

Jordan squatted on the wooden bed, still above the level of the rising ocean. She trembled uncontrollably as she shook her head. "It's always been dry."

Much as Maggie longed to wrap her arms around her daughter to offer comfort, she knew the water would surge through the opening as soon as she stepped away.

"Then he must have done something to cause this after he left me here."

"Jaime?"

"Jul—Yes, Jaime." Maggie racked her brain for a reason as to why the cave was suddenly filling with water. "Maybe there was some mechanism that diverted the tide. Whatever it was, it's not working now."

"He wanted us to die."

Maggie thought of offering her daughter platitudes, but the time had long since passed that she could keep Jordan safe from the real world. Maggie offered a wan smile. "I think he did. Yes."

"Bastard," Jordan muttered under breath. "Bastard!" she yelled.

Maggie chose not to correct the language. As far as she was concerned, the moniker was more than appropriate.

She stared up at the hole in the ceiling, wondering why Julian would have left it untouched. She studied the opening's diameter. Would she or Jordan be able to shimmy through if the water hoisted them that high?

Where there's a will, there's a way.

She smiled, awash suddenly in images of these past few days together with Will. As surreal as the news of his survival had been, seeing him alive, touching him, loving him, had been the happiest moments she'd experienced since the day Jordan was born.

If there was a way through that hole, she'd find it. She had no intention of dying without telling Will how she felt. Just as she had no intention of Jordan not surviving to be reunited with her father.

Daylight faded in the sky beyond, but if Maggie wasn't mistaken, on either side of the hole, there was another opening, a sliver of light. Could it be some sort of door?

She pointed. "Jordan, did you see the light to either side of the hole?"

Jordan tipped her head, her expression puzzled, but she gave no indication she'd heard her mother's question. Maggie's pulse thrummed in her ears.

Had she been stricken somehow? "Did you hear me —"

Jordan gave a sharp shake of her head. "Shh."

Maggie blinked, stunned by her daughter's tone of voice.

"Did you hear that?" Jordan asked, standing straight.

"What?"

"Voices." Jordan looked up at the hole as if she expected someone to look back. "I heard them last night. I heard someone say 'Maggie'."

Maggie's pulse kicked up a notch. "Just now?"

Jordan shook her head. "Last night. I mean, I think it was last night."

Last night?

Last night Maggie, Will and the others had been tracking Doc. Was this cave in the same part of the island? Had Jordan been so close they might have rescued her last night?

And then she heard it. One voice. Will's voice, calling out from the depths of the cave. But how could he be in the cave without drowning?

"Jordan! Maggie!"

"Will?" She shifted her weight and the board gave way, sending her stumbling into the water with a splash.

The water level increased at a frantic pace and Maggie sloshed through the now knee-deep water toward Jordan, reaching out her hand as she climbed on top of the wooden slab.

"We're getting out of here."

Jordan's eyes grew wide. She slipped her hand inside Maggie's and they clung to each other, the water rising quickly above their ankles, above their knees.

"We're both in great shape," Maggie said, nervous energy pulsing through her. "We can tread water once it's too deep for us to stand. We'll be all right."

"What if I can't?"

She gripped Jordan's shoulders, looking intently into her daughter's eyes. Will's eyes. "You can."

"But if I can't? What's going to happen then?"

Maggie pulled her daughter into her arms, tucking her head against her neck just as she used to do when Jordan was a young girl.

"Then I'll hold you up. For as long as it takes."

WILL AND Rick pressed forward along a narrow ledge, watching the water level below them steadily rise.

Will pressed the call button on his communicator. Silvia answered instantly.

"Get me the high-tide timing for this cove."

A split second later she answered. "Twenty more minutes, Will."

Twenty more minutes?

If they didn't find Maggie and Jordan soon, there was a very real possibility he and Rick wouldn't be able to get back out the way they came in.

"Any word from Kyle and Lily?" he asked.

"Just buzzed in. Your signals are visible on their trackers. They're about two hundred yards north of you and moving in. You should be within radio contact shortly."

"Excellent. Thanks."

In the moment Will let go of his communicator, he heard something. Based on the way Rick stilled, he'd heard the same.

"Voice," Rick said.

And then it came again. *"Bastard."*

"Maggie?" Rick asked.

Will shook his head, flashing back on the memory of Maggie at a younger age, the softer lilt of her voice, the slightly higher pitch. His pulse roared in his ears. "Jordan."

But who was she calling a bastard? Had Julian had a partner other than Doc? Was someone with his daughter now?

Unless the cave was playing tricks on their ears—a very real possibility—Jordan had called out from behind them somewhere.

"We've got to turn around."

But Rick was already in motion, scrambling toward the direction of the faint voice.

"Maggie! Jordan!" Will called out.

"Will?" An answering voice sounded.

Maggie.

Will focused so intently on the sound of his wife's voice, he almost missed the sensation of a surface other than rock when the side of his hand brushed something.

"Hold up." He alerted Rick to his change in pace as he scanned the area around his hand, working to focus his eyes in the dark, tight quarters.

And then he saw it.

A human skeleton.

A young girl. King's words bounced through his head.

Julian. Montoya's son. As heartless and cruel as his father had been.

Will swallowed down his anger and vowed to retrieve the skeleton after Jordan and Maggie were safe.

Somewhere on Cielo, a mother and father still grieved, still wondered, needed answers. The Body Hunters provided closure, even if the outcome wasn't always what the body's family had hoped for.

Right now, Will needed closure of his own. He stole one last glance at the skeleton as he and Rick shifted carefully on the ledge, heading back toward the direction of the voices.

Will's radio squawked and he spoke into his receiver. "Kyle?"

Relief washed through Will at the sound of Kyle's voice. They were moving in. "We can hear you, Will. Were you yelling?"

Will nodded but realized the move was useless. "I called to Maggie and Jordan. We heard someone, we think it's them. Are you picking anything up?"

"I'm picking you up. You've switched directions?"

"Affirmative."

"We're fifty yards from you, if that."

"Will!" Maggie's voice sounded again, this time louder, closer and full of panic.

"Sonofa—"

The radio went silent and Will's heart hammered in his chest. "Move faster," he called out to Rick.

"If you want to survive long enough to rescue your family, we've got to keep things steady," Rick answered.

Will wondered momentarily if he sounded as asinine as Rick when he kicked into control mode.

At that moment, he decided control was overrated.

From here on out, he'd be operating on good old-fashioned adrenaline and fast thinking.

"Kyle?" he yelled into the communicator. "Do you read me?"

The tiny device squawked again. Kyle sounded breathless when he spoke. "Lily's got a read on the voice. We're almost there."

Will waited, holding his breath as he crawled forward. His patience lasted no more than a few seconds. "Kyle?"

He heard Kyle's voice, suddenly, but the other agent wasn't speaking to him. He was speaking to Lily.

He'd left his radio open, and Will could hear everything.

"There's a door," Lily cried out. "It's rusted shut."

A muffled voice. No. *Voices.*

"Maggie? Jordan?" Kyle now.

Will's pulse raced through his veins, making him momentarily light-headed. He and Rick had to be close to wherever Kyle and Lily were. But he saw no signs of another entrance. No sign of a passage. No room. Nothing.

"Kyle?" he called out again.

"They're in rising water, Will. And you're almost directly below us now. You have to be close. We can't get this door open."

"A door?"

"Trapdoor," Kyle answered. "I'll leave the radio open, but they're in water over their heads and treading. I've got to get them out of there."

Water over their heads.

"How can you see them if the door's closed?"

"It's got a circular window."

"Big enough to get them through?"

"Negative."

"Keep at that door, then. We'll search for an entrance from this side."

And then Will heard it.

Rick stopped moving and Will did the same.

They listened, the sound of splashing unmistakable.

"Jordan, honey. Hang on. Jordan!" Maggie's voice.

"She's unconscious." Lily's voice.

"Kick, Maggie. Keep kicking." Kyle's voice. "Keep

her face above the water. I almost have the hinges off."

"Help me," Maggie cried out, the desperation in her voice reaching deep inside Will.

He had to reach her. Help her. Save her. Save Jordan.

Panic pushed Will forward and he climbed over Rick.

He'd find a way through this damned wall if it were the last thing he did.

CHAPTER EIGHTEEN

Body Clock: 84:45

"Kick, Maggie. Kick!" The urgency in Kyle's voice was something Maggie hadn't heard in the few days she'd known the man. "Keep kicking. I'm almost there."

Maggie kicked, fighting to keep Jordan's face above water.

"Wake up, baby." She sputtered against the rising ocean. "Jordan. Hang on. Just hang on."

Maggie lost her grip momentarily and Jordan slipped through her arms. Maggie dropped below the surface, anchoring her arms beneath Jordan's armpits, kicking with all of her might, pushing Jordan as high as she could, struggling to reach their shrinking pocket of air.

Panic squeezed at her chest, her need to breathe urgent. She knew better, and fought her body's natural urge to inhale. If she took a breath now, she'd take in nothing but water, and she wasn't about to drown. Not today.

Something crashed above her and the circle of light became a square—a blessedly large square.

Kyle had pried the trapdoor open.

Maggie relaxed, gulping down a mouthful of sea water.

She sputtered, gasping for breath, fighting to keep afloat, fighting to push Jordan toward the light.

Two silhouettes shimmered above the waterline. Kyle and Lily. They'd save Jordan. If only Maggie could push her high enough.

She summoned up her last ounce of strength, kicking furiously. In the moment Jordan cleared the surface, her weight was lifted from Maggie's arms.

Maggie relaxed again, gulping for air and finding none.

She swallowed another mouthful of water, then another. Choking. Sinking. Floating. Kicking.

Panic swirled through her and she let go of the struggle momentarily, letting a sense of peace wash through her.

She kept her focus on the square of light above, even though it faded farther and farther away.

Kyle's silhouette vanished from sight but then reappeared, reaching for her. Reaching.

Shouting. Reaching.

Surrounded by the fading glow of daylight, he

faded, growing dimmer and dimmer, farther and farther away.

"Maggie!"

Someone yelled.

Will.

Maggie smiled, a sudden sense of calm settling in her every bone and muscle.

He'd come. He hadn't left them alone after all. He'd found them just in time.

She stopped kicking and relaxed.

She didn't have to kick anymore.

Why should she?

Will was here now.

WILL'S FINGERS found the opening, slick where water spilled around the bottom edge of a large stone fitted perfectly into a hatch cut into the wall.

He and Rick worked to pull the stone free.

Water spilled onto the ledge and Rick turned away, hurling the stone behind them.

Will clambered to the opening, shoving his head and shoulders through the tight space.

No more than a foot of space sat between the water and the ceiling.

Kyle plucked Jordan from Maggie's arm, hoisting her through the opening to the outside.

Relief flooded through Will, replaced by horror as Maggie disappeared below the surface.

"Maggie!" He screamed her name, even as he shimmied farther through the opening, determined to break through, even though he was now wedged in tightly, his ribs screaming with the pressure.

"Maggie!" he called out again.

He saw no motion. No kicking. No flailing.

Nothing but the smooth surface of the rising water.

He hadn't come this far to lose her now.

"I've got you," Rick yelled as he pushed against Will's backside.

Will drew in a deep breath as his body slipped through the hole. Hope surged through him as he slid into the water, murky with years of accumulated dust and sand. He opened his eyes, but saw nothing.

Operating on sheer instinct, he kicked furiously to a spot directly below the trapdoor above. He hit the stone floor, running his hands in every direction, feeling the water around him, above him, beside him.

When he connected with flesh, he grabbed on, pulling Maggie to his chest, holding her tightly as he kicked toward the illuminated square above, ignoring the crushing ache in his lungs and his body's need to inhale.

He thrust Maggie into Kyle's waiting hands then grabbed for the sides of the opening, greedily gulping air into his lungs.

"Rick?" he asked as he climbed through the opening, and scrambled to his feet.

"Behind you, buddy."

He gave Rick a hand, pulling him through the trapdoor, then rushed to Maggie's side.

Kyle administered mouth-to-mouth and Maggie's response was instant. She coughed out two mouthfuls of water and opened her eyes, twisting to her side, frantically searching for their daughter.

"Jordan?" She spoke so weakly she was barely audible.

"She'll be all right," Lily answered as she cradled Jordan in her lap. "You saved her. She didn't take on any water."

Will froze momentarily at the sight of his daughter, unconscious but breathing. Grown-up. Beautiful. So close he could touch her.

"Go ahead." Maggie had pulled herself to her knees and gestured for Will to go to Jordan.

Will reached for Maggie first, cupping her face in his hands. "You're all right?"

She pressed a quick kiss to his lips. "I am now." She tipped her head toward Jordan. "Let your daughter know you're here."

He scrambled to where Jordan lay, easing her head onto his lap, stroking her damp cheek, brushing back the wet strands of long blond hair identical to her mother's.

"Emergency crews are on their way." Lily stood, moving toward Kyle and Rick to give Will and his family space.

He shot her a grateful smile, then looked down at his daughter. His beautiful daughter.

"Hey, baby," he said softly, swallowing down the lump in his throat.

"Dad?" Jordan's eyes blinked open. "You came for us."

"And I'm not going anywhere ever again."

As quickly as Jordan regained consciousness, she

lost it again. A siren sounded in the distance, drawing nearer.

Will brushed a hand across Jordan's cheek, reached for Maggie's hand and then waited with his family.

Together, at last.

CHAPTER NINETEEN

Body Clock: 88:00

Status: Alive

After the throng of medical personnel had left Jordan's exam room, Will slipped in unnoticed, lowering himself to the chair next to his daughter's bed. He pulled himself as close to her as possible and watched her sleep.

The hospital wanted to keep her for a day or two, but she'd make a full recovery, suffering only from mild dehydration and some bruising. Amazingly, she'd suffered no serious injuries or broken bones during her ordeal.

Maggie had been treated and was in the process of being released. She'd promised to meet Will when she was finished with her paperwork.

A feeling of peace overcame him, easing through every inch of his body even as exhaustion pushed at the edges of his awareness.

After seventeen years, the threat of Diego Montoya was dead and buried. Maggie and Jordan were safe—truly safe—at last.

The rainbow quilt lay tucked into Jordan's arms, and Will smiled. Silvia had been at the hospital waiting for them upon arrival.

He reached out to touch the tangible symbol of his team's faith and love, and Jordan stirred.

"Dad?" Her brown eyes opened slowly and she smiled.

"Right here." He patted her hand. "How are you feeling?"

"Sleepy."

"Then rest." He took her hand, jolted by the overwhelming sense of coming home that passed through him. "I'll stay right here."

"What about the skeleton?" Jordan's lovely features crumpled with concern as she whispered the question.

So word had spread about their find in the cave.

"A local girl who disappeared back when Julian..." Will hesitated. "...Jaime was a boy."

Jordan's throat worked. "He killed her?"

"Appears so." Will studied the fresh wave of fear that washed across his daughter's face and squeezed her hand. "He'll never hurt anyone again, honey. Not ever."

She stared into his eyes, seeming to search for

something, studying him intently.

Typically such moments of silence would have made Will uncomfortable, but his daughter's scrutiny was anything but.

"Will you go away again now?" Jordan finally asked.

Her words cut him, grounding him in the moment. "I'll leave that up to you."

Jordan blinked. "What do you mean?"

Will tightened his grip on her hand, the hand he'd last held when she was a toddler first learning to walk. He couldn't bear the thought of losing her now, but he'd respect her wishes. He wouldn't force himself on a family that didn't want him.

"I mean, you're a young woman now. You have a say in what happens next. I'm nothing more than a stranger to you."

Jordan smiled, moisture glistening in her eyes. "I used to imagine what you'd be like, if you were alive." She swallowed, her voice tight. "And I was exactly right." She gave a quick shake of her head. "I don't want to have to imagine anymore, Dad."

Will gathered her into his arms, careful not to hurt her. "I love you, Jordan. I always have."

"I love you, too, Dad."

Maggie cleared her throat from the doorway. "Don't I have a say in this?"

Jordan pulled herself to a sitting position and Will stood, watching the play of emotions on Maggie's face.

She reached into her pocket as she crossed the room to take Will's hand, pressing his ring into his palm. "I believe this belongs to you."

He held the plain gold band between his thumb and forefinger, turning to Jordan. "I understand you wore this around your neck."

"Your wedding band. You found it." His daughter beamed. "I always knew it would bring me luck."

Will's heart swelled with pride and love for his beautiful wife and the young woman his daughter had become. He held out the ring in Jordan's direction, but she held up a hand.

"You wear it, Daddy."

Daddy.

One last pocket of restraint and control burst inside him, shattering the need to guard his emotions, to deny his feelings. He handed the ring to Maggie and she took his hand in hers, gliding the gold band onto his ring finger, never taking her eyes from his.

"Still fits," she said softly.

And as he stared into her eyes, he spotted a flash of undeniable love and happiness.

Still fits.

He pulled his wife into his arms and reached for Jordan's hand. "Always," he said, feeling at home for the first time in seventeen years. "Always."

MAGGIE BIT BACK her tears, overcome by the sight of her husband's wedding band on his finger, where the ring had always belonged. "I have to ask you something."

Will lifted his focus to her expectantly.

"The album." She choked on the words, losing her

battle to keep her emotions at bay.

Will cupped her face in his hands and shook his head. "Just because I wasn't the one to put the album together doesn't mean I didn't want to."

"Then why didn't you?"

He gave a slight smile, and Maggie suddenly saw how difficult the admission he was about to make was for him.

"Because I knew I wouldn't be able to stay away if I saw you again."

"Would that have been so wrong?"

"I love you, Maggie. Too much to risk your life."

"So you walked away and never looked back?"

Will nodded. "I'd rather think of you alive and happy than dead because of me."

Will sank his fingers into her thick hair, pulling her mouth to his. Maggie braced her palms against his chest, pushing him away.

"Would you do it again?"

"What?"

Impatience flickered to life inside her. "You know what."

"All of it?" he asked.

She nodded.

Something lit deep within Will's eyes, a resignation she'd caught a glimpse of once or twice before, but that now shone back at her without a trace of doubt.

He thinned his lips. "I would."

But instead of asking him to leave, instead of walking away and never looking back, Maggie stood her ground, toe to toe with the man she'd lost once, the man she never wanted to lose again.

She studied the love shining in his gaze, the stubbornness, the fearlessness, the countless emotions washing across his tired features and she understood.

For the first time in seventeen years, Maggie understood exactly why Will did what he did.

Tears blurred her vision. In that instant she knew she'd have made the same choice, given the same set of circumstances. She also knew she was ready to go home.

With Jordan.

With Will.

As the family they'd once been—the family they'd be once more. Altered. A bit damaged, no doubt, but a family nonetheless.

Their family.

Her family.

"Damn you, Will Connor." The corners of her mouth pulled into a soft smile.

Will's own grin spread wide as he pulled her into his arms, his lips brushing against her ear, sending a shiver down her spine. "You always did say the sweetest things, Maggie Connor."

A laugh slid between Maggie's lips. "And I always will."

EPILOGUE

Ten days later, the Body Hunters stood at the back of the island funeral out of respect for the dead girl and her family.

The skeletal remains from the cave had been identified as the young girl missing since she'd been abducted by Julian years earlier.

The girl's parents had been grateful to finally close the most painful chapter of their lives. They sat at the grave-side to say their goodbyes, surrounded by friends and family, including Adele Jones.

Mrs. Jones had returned to her home after news of Julian's death had spread. He'd run her out of town with his threats, but in an uncommon act of decency, had left her unharmed.

Commissioner Dunkley had not been so fortunate. Upon Will's inquiry, the Royal Cielo Police had found their commissioner's body just inside the front door to his home, a single gunshot wound between his eyes. The leather cord from Jordan's necklace had never been found, but Will and Maggie had found something even better to replace it with.

Eileen Caldwell had resigned her position as resort manager and planned to return home to Pittsburgh. Apparently she'd decided she'd hidden from her family's ghosts long enough. And although the attractive brunette had already said her goodbyes to the team, the stolen glances between her and Kyle hadn't been lost on Will.

Ferdinand King had fled Cielo as promised. Even though he'd gone underground, the man had arranged for Julian's remains to be buried in their rightful place in the Montoya family plot. Rumor had it the vase on Isabel Montoya's grave, however, sat empty once more.

Just as Will had suspected, Julian had sabotaged the sea gates leading to the cave, jamming the switches that prevented the ocean's high tide from filling the numerous passageways and crevices.

Additionally, he'd outfitted the entrance to the chamber with a piece of particleboard, guaranteed to buckle and collapse when wet.

He'd thought of everything to seal Jordan and Maggie's fate before he'd left to meet Will at the Abbey. But he'd forgotten the power of two things.

The determination of a family to survive and the Body Hunters' vow to bring the body home alive.

As the mourners began to trickle back to their cars, Jordan walked toward the grieving parents, her treasured quilt bundled into her arms. She'd asked Silvia if she could present the quilt as a gesture of sympathy, and Silvia had been quick to say yes. Jordan placed the quilt in the mother's arms, gave the woman a hug, then turned, headed straight for Will and Maggie.

Will couldn't have been more proud, both of Jordan and of Maggie, who had raised their daughter all alone.

Jordan traced her finger over her new necklace, a trio of interwoven gold bands, hanging from a slender chain.

She caught him watching and smiled.

Will's heart swelled. He didn't think he'd ever grow tired of watching the young woman Jordan had become. He gave Maggie's hand a squeeze, and she leaned into him, her body warm against his.

They were scheduled to fly back to Seattle later that day on a commercial flight.

Three seats across.

Family style.

The rest of the Body Hunters team would head back to their lives, where they'd wait until a new case called. And when a new body clock began to tick, they'd go where they were needed.

After all, that's what the Body Hunters did.

Don't miss these exciting Body Hunters titles:

Silenced

Shattered

ABOUT THE AUTHOR

USA Today and Wall Street Journal bestseller Kathleen Long is the author of nineteen novels in the genres of women's fiction, suspense, and fiction for young readers. A native of Wilmington, Delaware, and a graduate of the University of Delaware, she divides her time between suburban Philadelphia and the Jersey shore. When Kathleen is not hiding in a corner of the local library writing her next book, she spends her time bribing her teen to take off her headphones, begging the dog to heel, and teaching creative writing.

Please visit her at www.kathleenlong.com.

BOOKS IN THIS SERIES

Body Hunters

If you love fast-paced romantic suspense, you'll devour the heart-pounding Body Hunters series from USA TODAY bestseller, Kathleen Long.

Gone

In a race against a killer, can two desperate parents save their daughter before time runs out?

The Body Clock is ticking.

Maggie Connor will do whatever it takes to find her missing daughter, but what if that means working alongside the husband she "buried" seventeen years earlier? In order to save his family, Will faked his own death, and he'll stop at nothing to bring his daughter home now. Maggie and Will's reunion ignites an undeniable anger—and an unmistakable passion—but will they find the killer before it's too late?

Silenced

Body Hunter Lily Christides never imagined she'd one day be chasing her sister's killer. But when investigative reporter Nicole Christides is murdered shortly after helping overturn a killer's sentence, that's exactly where Lily finds herself.

Philadelphia detective Cameron Hughes never dreamed the man he worked so hard to convict would one day walk free. When Nicole Christides is found murdered, Cam is determined to put Buddy Grey back where he belongs. Behind bars.

Lily believes Grey is innocent. Cam plans to prove his guilt.

When the killer makes it known Lily is next on his list, she and Cam begin a race against the clock. Will they unmask the murderer before time runs out? Or will the truth be silenced forever?

Shattered

When hotel manager Eileen Caldwell leaves Isle de Cielo to return to the life she left behind, she never imagined she'd walk into her past. Literally. After working to escape the mystery of her older brother's disappearance and suicide, she now finds herself searching again, this time for her younger brother, vanished in exactly the same way. Has history repeated itself? Or is there time to save this life, avoiding the outcome that's haunted her dreams—and nightmares—for the past five years?

Kyle Landenburg has tried to forget the hotel manager who turned his head during the Body Hunters' Cielo investigation. Blaming himself for the death of the only woman he ever loved, he's vowed never to let his emotions again be vulnerable, yet he hasn't been able to shake the impact Eileen Caldwell blazed across his memory and his heart.

When the Body Hunters take on the case of her missing brother, he'll use his intuition and skills to do whatever it takes to bring the man home alive. But when the past turns out to be far more complicated than anyone ever imagined and the present becomes a maze of dead-end clues and life-threatening twists, he'll be fighting more than the romantic tension building between him and Eileen. He'll be fighting an invisible foe determined that this time Eileen's family will be shattered...forever.